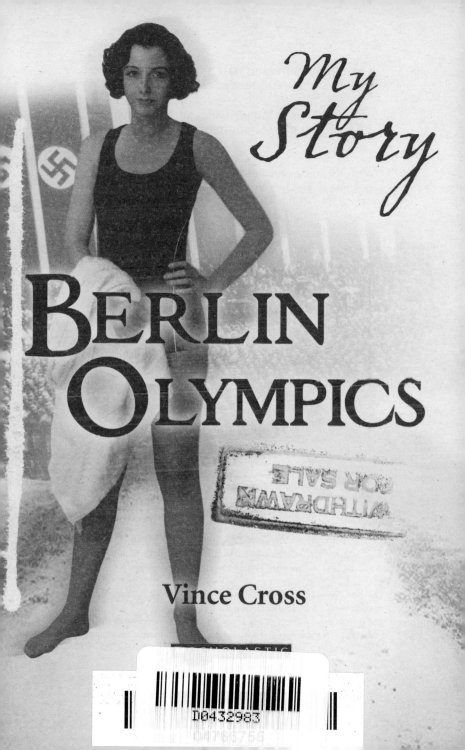

My Story

BERLIN OLYMPICS

Vince Cross

SCHOLASTIC

For the students and staff of the North London
Collegiate School.

With thanks to Wendy Coles and the Amateur
Swimming Association for their assistance.

While the events described and some of the characters in this
book may be based on actual historical events and real people,
Eleanor Rhys Davies is a fictional character, created by the author,
and her story is a work of fiction.

Scholastic Children's Books
Euston House, 24 Eversholt Street,
London, NW1 1DB, UK

A division of Scholastic Ltd
London ~ New York ~ Toronto ~ Sydney ~ Auckland
Mexico City ~ New Delhi ~ Hong Kong

Published in the UK by Scholastic Ltd, 2012

Text copyright © Vince Cross, 2012
Cover illustration © Richard Jones, 2012

ISBN 978 1407 13035 4

Printed and bound by CPI Group (UK) Ltd, Croydon, CR0 4YY

2 4 6 8 10 9 7 5 3 1

The right of Vince Cross to be identified as the author of
this work has been asserted by him in accordance with the
Copyright, Designs and Patents Act, 1988.

Saturday 29th June 1935

Miss Wilson says I should keep a diary. She says if I put half as much effort into my English lessons as I do into my swimming I'd be the next Virginia Woolf, whoever she is. So to keep her sweet, and because I suppose one day it might be nice to read about me when I was fourteen, here goes.

Today I went to the Jubilee party for King George down on Hale Lane. Just about everyone we know was there. With all its new housing I suppose Edgware's a real town now and definitely not a village, but that's the way I still think of it, from when I was very small and we'd just moved back from Islington to get away from the smoke and grime of London. They'd laid out tables right there on the paved circle in front of the station, while the trams and cars kept driving by, and there were a lot of speeches including one from my father, because of him being warden at St Margaret's church. There was a brass band, which played the National Anthem very loudly right in my ear, and we had a jolly tea. I ate more cake and jelly than I should have, but it doesn't matter. I can always starve myself for a couple of days. Anyway, it's true what Mother says, I don't put on an ounce of weight however much I eat. Even when I'm not swimming, I never stop moving. That's me: a cat on a hot tin roof.

Grandpa was already fifty and the Great War was still four years in the future when George the Fifth was crowned king back in 1910. And Father was born in Grandpa's huge old house up on the hill at Stanmore when Queen Victoria was still on the throne. He remembers from when he was little how they celebrated her Diamond Jubilee in exactly the same way we did today. There were no cars in the muddy streets then and only occasional steam trains puffed their way into the old station (the new electric 'tube' line arrived in Edgware in 1924, just before we came back). In Queen Victoria's time the whole village could sit at the tables they laid out. As Father said in his speech, 'how things have changed'. But he thinks they've all changed for the worse, and the whole world is going to the dogs. I don't agree with him one bit. I think at least some things have changed much for the better, and the bright new modern world is wonderful. For instance next year the nasty clanking old trams are going to disappear, and we'll have smart shiny trolley-buses instead. And two years ago, they built the Ritz cinema near the station, which was a big improvement and lucky for us.

I suppose I should tell you who I am, shouldn't I, or is that silly, since no one but me will probably ever read this? Well, let's pretend someone's going to.

I'm Eleanor Angharad Rhys Davies, and I'm so lucky

2

because I live in Seymour Lodge which is a lovely big modern house on the Canons Estate – that's just near the park to the west of Edgware. Grandpa sold the grand old haunted mansion in Stanmore five years ago and lives with us now. My father is William Rhys Davies, and you can probably guess from my name and his that there's Welsh blood in our veins, although to hear us talk you wouldn't know it. I think we probably just sound posh. My mother is Isobel Eileen, and you already know about Grandpa. Apart from that we have a housekeeper, Mrs Etheridge, and a maid called Amy. Amy lives in a room at the top of the house, and Mrs Etheridge has a little house down in the village with her husband Bert, who does our garden. Bert has a wooden leg. He lost the real one during the war. Father does something very important for the government at the Foreign Office in Whitehall, although I'm not sure quite what. He starts work very early and often isn't home till seven. Even then the telephone sometimes rings in the evenings or weekends with someone wanting to speak to him urgently.

I'm an only child. I shouldn't have been, but my elder brother Emrys died when he was three and I was still a very little baby. My mother had such a bad time with me that she said no more, thank you, after that. My best friend is Sarah Rosenthal and she lives in one of the arty new houses with steel-framed curved windows up in Stonegrove. We go to school together every day which means catching the tube train from Edgware station at a quarter to eight and then getting off at Mornington Crescent, which is almost in the middle of London, after a rattling, bumping journey of nearly half an hour. Our school is the Camden Collegiate School, or CCS, and it's supposed to be top-drawer. The best thing as far as I'm concerned is that CCS is situated right next to the St Pancras swimming baths, so Sarah and I get to practise our swimming there most days, rain or shine.

Sunday 7th July 1935

Something smashing to write at last, and a real adventure too, even if it's going to make me sound big-headed. Yesterday Sarah and I went to the National Schools Swimming Championships in Hastings, at the new St Leonard's Lido. A trip to the seaside and a swimming competition all rolled into one!

We knew we were going to have to get up really early, so Sarah stayed at our house on Friday night. As per instructions we met Mrs Williams our swimming teacher outside CCS on the dot of half past seven yesterday morning. Then it was off to Charing Cross station to catch the Hastings train which got us into St Leonard's at about eleven. We just had time to go and eat our sandwiches on an absolutely freezing sea-front before registering for our events. I was going to swim the quarter-mile freestyle and Sarah the 220 yards breast stroke.

The St Leonard's lido is huge. When you stand there waiting for your race to start, the lido stretches out into the distance, and yesterday they were using only half of it – just up to the diving boards which hang out over the middle of the pool. From outside it reminded me of pictures I've seen of the Colosseum in Rome, and yet because it's built of concrete it manages to look modern at the same time. There's a tiered bank of seats all the way down the side furthest from the sea, although there weren't many people watching us yesterday. A bit sore on the old bottom I should think, if you were sitting there all afternoon.

Anyway, it was so imposing I had butterflies in my tum right from the moment we walked in, and I told Mrs Williams so. Now I like Mrs Williams, but she's rather a 'no nonsense' sort of woman. If it had been my mother there, she'd have sympathized and told me I was a poor darling and not to mind: I'd be able to cope. Mrs Williams just sort of harrumphed and said, "Good. A few nerves never did a girl any harm."

Thank goodness the lido was sheltered from the cold wind, but it was still pretty chilly for early July.

"Keep loose and warmed up, ladies," said Mrs Williams.

"Easy to pull a muscle on a day like this. Come on now! Stretch! Keep moving. Run on the spot!"

There were only eight competitors for the quarter-mile, so I wasn't going to be 'on' till half past four, but Sarah had to swim a heat just to make the final. There were going to be three heats with the first two from each heat plus the two fastest losers battling it out later on.

"They're all huge," she muttered, looking at the other girls, and she was absolutely spot on. Neither of us is exactly short, but a couple of them must have been nearly six foot in their bare feet and broad in the beam to boot. I'm a beanpole. Sarah's more of a sturdy sapling. I'm fair(ish!)-haired and she's dark.

"All fat and no form," I lied gamely. "Think of having to pull all that weight through the water."

Secretly I was thinking, "Poor Sarah. She's got no chance…"

I needn't have worried. Actually, there wasn't any form to speak of in Sarah's heat, and she swam an easy last length for a comfortable second place. But it was obvious that at least one of the other heats was much faster, and when it came to the final later in the afternoon, Sarah was a distant fourth. When she pulled herself out of the water, I could see she was disappointed.

"Jolly well done," said Mrs Williams encouragingly. "You've got to remember, Sarah, some of those girls were a couple of years older than you. You shouldn't be swimming

6

breast stroke anyway: you should be giving young Eleanor here a run for her money in the longer freestyle events."

"She was just being nice," Sarah said disconsolately. "She had to say something cheerful, didn't she? She couldn't very well say I was hopeless."

"Is Mrs Williams ever nice for the sake of it?" I said, trying to buck her up. "I don't think that's the way you get to be a selector for the National Team."

Twenty past four came round, and I presented myself at the pool side for my moment of glory – or ignominy.

"Now we'll see what you're made of," said Mrs Williams. "You know who that is, don't you?" She pointed at a well-built girl on the far side in Lane Seven.

I shook my head, teeth chattering with cold and nerves.

"That's Margaret Jeffrey. National standard swimmer. She's the one to beat."

When the gun went, I swam out fast, probably too fast. I think I may even have been leading after a couple of lengths – at any rate I couldn't see anyone to my immediate left or right – and I was aware of a lot of noise as I turned for the second time. But by halfway, I was really beginning to feel it in my legs, and towards the end I felt as if I was swimming backwards. After I'd touched, I'd no idea where I'd come – probably last, I thought miserably.

I hauled myself onto the side, and pulled off my swimming cap.

"Not half bad, carrot top," said a tomboyish girl with an extremely posh voice. "Topping swim and all that..."

"I beg your pardon," I said, not in a mood to be insulted as well as humiliated. There's just a suggestion of auburn in my hair, but in no way do I resemble a carrot.

"Think you came second to the Jeffrey girl," she said, completely oblivious to the fact I was a bit put out.

"Did I?" I answered with all the grace I could muster. "Gosh!"

"Six minutes and ten seconds," said Mrs Williams, waving her stopwatch quite excitedly, I thought. "You've excelled yourself, Ellie. And you gave young Margaret a jolly good fright. In an outside pool too. Well done!"

I haven't come down from the ceiling since!

Wednesday 10th July 1935

Miss Wilson nabbed me after English today, smiled, and asked, "How's that diary of yours coming along, Eleanor?"

Having only made two entries in a fortnight – as you know – I made a sort of 'so-so' face.

"Do you want to read it?" I asked nervously. The answer I wanted was 'no'.

"Do *you* want me to read it?" she replied. I probably shrugged and looked sheepish.

"Look, Eleanor," she said, "please don't take this the wrong way, but I've got plenty of marking to do, without checking up on you all the time. You're a CCS girl. This is about self-discipline. I just thought you might find writing a diary fun. Sometimes diaries help us understand ourselves better. Don't make life difficult for yourself. Just write about what happens during an ordinary day."

"That sounds boring!" I found myself saying.

"Are you a boring person, Eleanor?" she asked.

"S'pose not, Miss Wilson," I muttered.

"No, exactly. You strike me as a very unboring person. So just let that lively mind of yours find its way onto paper. If you write from the heart it'll never be boring, I promise!"

I have to admit it, of all the teachers at CCS, and even above Mrs Williams, Miss Wilson is very good at making you feel nice.

So. Eleanor's ordinary day. Well, I always sleep like a log so the day starts when my alarm clock wakes me at half past six. I wash and then throw on our bottle-green school uniform (extra quickly in winter because the house gets so cold – there's often ice inside the windows), and eat the breakfast Amy has made for Mother and me. Amy isn't very good with suppers yet – Mrs Etheridge does dinner for us most nights – but her bacon and eggs are all right. I grab my horrible school panama hat (green and grey ribbon), leaving the house at twenty past seven exactly, and run off to meet Sarah outside the station. It's a pleasant perambulation down beside the pond, between the grand columns by the estate lodge, along the High Street, past the war memorial and the old half-timbered houses. Then it's up Hale Lane, and into the station.

When we arrive at Mornington Crescent it's a brisk or dawdling walk to CCS, depending on the time, and straight into our class for registration at 8.40 before assembly. At this point Sarah and I go our separate ways because Sarah's Jewish and they have their own bash. There are barely a dozen Jewish girls, and it seems a good wheeze to me, because they don't get harangued like the rest of us do about good manners and school uniform (skirts must be no more and no less than three inches from the floor when kneeling, girls!) and what a good CCS pupil should be doing with her free time in the evenings and at weekends (i.e. no trips to the Ritz Cinema, or listening to the wireless or going to parties or indeed having any fun at all!) and The Importance of Homework. As far as I can make out, after their prayers and what have you, the Jewish girls just have a jolly natter for ten minutes with nice pink and plump Miss Abrahams, who teaches us all mystifying mathematics. Except once a week when they have to come back and join us for a major lecture on Cleanliness being next to Godliness or How a Camden Gal can Conquer the World.

10

We have classes all through the morning until our heads spin, with a break for civilized milk and biscuits served by Doreen the school maid at eleven, and then lunch in the main hall at one o'clock, which costs two pounds ten shillings a term. Considering what gets dished up at lunchtime, that strikes me as outrageous -- as I keep telling Father, though he never listens. Then from half past one we do improving things, which sometimes might include private study or needlework (ugh!), except on Thursdays when we troop off up the road to play lacrosse, hockey or cricket depending on the term. As often as we can, Sarah, I and a couple of other girls whose parents don't think it unladylike spend the afternoons swimming under Mrs William's beady eye next door at the Baths, while other less sporty types dance, play the piano or sing. I am completely tone-deaf, so that's never been something that's interested me. In exams I always seem to languish in the bottom half of the class lists. This gets me sympathy from Mother but annoys Father hugely. I suppose that's because he's paying the school bills, and thinks he should be getting better value for his money. For all that he's an old fuddy-duddy in many ways, he has strong views about girls' education. He thinks we should be taught exactly the same as boys, and I do agree with him about that: it really annoys me when the brothers of my friends, including Sarah's, are so superior about everything. The teachers say I get easily bored, and it may be true. I don't really find anything they teach us very difficult – apart from the dreaded maths, and I confess, I'm easily distracted. During the last year or so there have been a couple of awkward conversations with our headmistress, Miss Bowes, about my lack of 'application'.

Miss Bowes' office is darkly decorated in chocolate brown. She holds herself primly at a high desk surrounded by pens and paper. A standard lamp shines out towards where her victim (i.e. me!) slumps, on a much lower chair, neck craning upwards, blinded by the light.

"Eleanor Davies," she says slowly, rolling the syllables around her mouth. "Eleanor Angharad Rhys Davies..."

She narrows her eyes over her round glasses, then takes them off and snaps them shut.

"A disappointment. A considerable disappointment. There's a lot of room for improvement. In so many ways. What are we going to do with you?"

Sometimes in summer before we catch the tube home, if Sarah and I have finished swimming early, we go up onto the parkland grass at Primrose Hill, and look down on the magic land of London laid out before us, the buildings, the traffic, the haze of smoke, the line of the river Thames. It's the modern world coming out to meet us in Edgware a bit more every day. Our parents thought they could escape from the city, but the city's growing so fast, filling in the gaps where the fields once were. The world is changing around us. What will it be like in another ten years time? Or another twenty, when we have families of our own? (Little shudder!) What a strange thought!

Back home after school, there's homework, maybe an hour if we're lucky, or two if we're not. Supper at our house is at seven, when Father comes home. It's a serious meal with a capital S, the three of us plus (sometimes) Grandpa alone together around the table, with compulsory discussion of the day's events. My father does a lot of the talking. Mother asks questions. I sometimes say what I think, with unpredictable results. Sometimes what I think gives Father a chance to start sounding off again. Sometimes we disagree, and he tells me I don't know what I'm talking about: I'll understand when I'm older. I think I understand some things very well now.

I go to bed at nine o'clock, as demanded by the rules and regulations of the Camden Collegiate School. Mother has to sign a note each day to say I have, and that I've done my homework. Anyway, according to Mother, I need my beauty sleep and nine hours is the minimum for beauty to be achieved at fourteen, apparently. Getting uglier by the minute, I read silly romantic novels under the blanket with a torch. Sarah and I club together to buy them with our pocket money. They are mostly books of which Miss Wilson and (particularly) Miss Bowes would not approve one jot. In fact, if they knew what we read in our spare time, there'd be an Assembly entirely devoted to how evil such things are.

Thursday 18th July 1935

Speech Day. Insufferably hot and sticky too. For this we are marched down to Westminster's Central Hall, in our best tussore silk dresses. We are wrung out with perspiration by the time we get there, and three girls fall off their chairs in a dead faint before we even start, but the school is on show to the world, which is after all what matters. We sit for hours while speeches are made in turn by the Chairman of Governors, Rev. Professor Lambert Whatmough D.D. M.C. F.R.S. etc. etc., whom no one can hear, by Miss Bowes whom we certainly all can, and finally and supposedly for the edification of us gals of Camden, by Miss Hilary Henrickson, who centuries ago attended CCS before going off to darkest Africa to be a famous missionary. However there are no exciting stories of cannibals and cooking pots or pygmies and pig-sticking. Just more haranguing: the evils of the cinema and dancing, a general decline in morals, and apparently we can no longer walk or talk properly.

This is particularly unhelpful to those of us who have to struggle out into the aisle and up onto the platform to collect our prizes. Those who are not dying of heatstroke are desperate for the lavatory after two hours of cross-legged boredom. In neither case can we walk straight.

I am to receive the School Swimming Prize, which turns out to be a very beautiful book of photographs entitled *The Art of Diving*. It's lovely but of course completely useless. Diving off any sort of board more than two inches off the ground scares me witless. How much more sensible it would be if they only let us choose something. But perhaps they're worried we might choose something soppy or trivial like Rose Gershwin's *It Started with a Kiss* or Graciela St John's *Three Days in Paris*. As if we would...

Sarah doesn't get a prize, and would have liked one, but she's a good egg about mine.

"Did I look a total zombie when I shook Henrickson's hand?" I ask afterwards.

"You looked fine," Sarah reassures me. "Perfectly normal."

"So I did look like a zombie..."

"Well, only a bit..."

Mrs Williams comes upon us before we rejoin my mother and Sarah's parents at the end of proceedings.

"Well done young Eleanor," she booms. "Hard luck Sarah. Your turn next time, I expect. I'm glad to have caught the two of you together. I wondered what you'd think of training with me at the Mermaid Club over the summer?"

The Mermaid is a very famous, posh, ladies' swimming club. A lot of the best British swimmers have been members.

This is a surprising invitation.

"Monday, Tuesday and Thursday evenings." she continues, at a volume which keeps most of Westminster informed about the proposal. "Five-thirty sharp at the Hampstead baths."

"Thank you very much," we stutter. "Of course our parents might..."

"I'll straighten them out," she says, as if there couldn't possibly be any doubt about the matter. "Just leave it to me. Thing is ... you might just have a future ... the both of you. Olympics next year. Y'never know. England expects and all that ..."

And she was off through the crowd leaving us stunned. "The Olympics!" said Sarah. "England expects! What is she going on about? Screw loose if you ask me!"

But it's got me thinking. How much would we have to improve to stand a chance of making the Olympic team? Is it such a silly idea? A lot of the top swimmers aren't so much older than us. Now, that wouldn't be boring. Not one bit.

Saturday 20th July 1935

It was still horribly hot today, and a huge thunderstorm brought a sudden and wet end to the St Margaret's horticultural show. Mr Etheridge did very well with the marrows and carrots he grows in our kitchen garden, and Mother swept the board with her flower arranging, but it wasn't much fun swanning around trying to look pretty in my best dress and hat as if it was Buckingham Palace rather than a local church 'do'. I missed Sarah's company. Just because I go to CCS there's a certain type of local Edgware brat that thinks I'm fair game. So today they were taking any opportunity to trip me up or spill ice cream on aforesaid best dress. And if they weren't doing that, then they were bribing their ragamuffin younger brothers into poking me in the ribs and shouting rude names. It's very tedious, but what can you do? I could've caught one of them and tweaked its ear or found a way of putting it down the church coal-hole, but that would only have got me into trouble, so it was just a trifling pain that had to be borne. The rain was a welcome relief, really.

Over dinner, Father said, as if to no one in particular,

"I had a letter this morning."

Mother and I continued trying to digest Amy's rather chewy lamb fillet. Grandpa was in his own little world. He very rarely joins in family conversation these days. He's a man of few words, and even then only some of them make sense.

"From the school..."

Now I had to pretend not to be interested. What had I done?

"Who is this Mrs Williams?" he asked truculently.

"You know who Mrs Williams is, dear," Mother said mildly. "She teaches Eleanor swimming."

"And why is she seeking to organize our family life for the next six weeks?"

Oh, that! I wanted to ask if there hadn't been anything in the newspapers worth arguing about today, but knew it would just make things worse. Darling Father clearly wanted to make a fuss about something, and he'd chosen this.

"Suppose we wish to go away? For a holiday, for instance."

"Have you arranged one, dear, and not told me about it? How nice!" said Mother with a smile. She knew very well he hadn't.

"One might wonder whether it was a good idea to have a daughter running around London at any time of day or night," Father mused, eyebrows bristling.

"It's nice, safe Hampstead. I've been there lots of times

on my own," I replied, trying hard not to rise to the bait. "Anyway I'll be with Sarah all the time. And we'll be back home before dark."

"That would be Miss Rosenthal..."

"Yes, Sarah Rosenthal."

"The Jewish family..."

"Yes, that Sarah," I answered impatiently. I don't like the way he keeps bringing this subject up. Father seems to have a thing about the growing number of Jews in Edgware.

"I'm not sure I think this obsession with swimming is altogether healthy," he tried. "Trivial ... and not very feminine."

"Surely very healthy, dear," my mother answered. "Aren't you always saying 'A healthy body in a healthy mind', William?"

"The other way round, last time I looked," he muttered, irked that Mother wasn't siding with him. "*Mens sana in corpore sano.*"

"And if science is good for girls," I added, "and maths, and geography, why not sport?"

"Unladylike," he grumbled. "Unladylike and distinctly unbecoming. I don't want my daughter flaunting herself in front of the whole world like a showgirl."

My mother only rarely takes my father on, but this was one occasion. She never has to say much to make her feelings clear.

"I think ..." she said, appearing to choose her words carefully, "... I think you sometimes need to be more careful about what you say, William, lest you cause hurt where you do not intend it."

There was a glum silence for a while until the dessert arrived and Father was able to get himself off the hook by saying approvingly, "We shall struggle to improve on the quality of last year's crop of plums, shan't we, my dear?"

After dinner, Mother said quietly to me, "It'll be all right, darling. You know your father. He just feels it's wrong to give in too easily. Try not to worry."

I hope she's right. I don't want to feel I'm going against his wishes. This is too important to me.

Wednesday 11th September 1935

A new school year. We are now the Upper Fifth form and almost grown up, and there's a new girl in our class too. Her name's Tara Macdonald, she's American – from the city of Boston, which I've just looked up on the map – and she's a swimmer too. Even better than that, she's funny and nice, and already after only two days, she, Sarah and I are great friends.

Miss Scaldwell, our form mistress, had obviously guessed we'd get on like a house on fire.

"Perhaps you could show Tara the ropes, Eleanor," she said. "I'm sure you two will find a lot to talk about. Just don't do it in my History lessons, please!

One thing I can't get over is how polite Tara is. It was all I could do to stop her calling me 'Miss Davies' at first.

"That's really nice," she said and blushed, when I said "Call me Ellie." "Thank you. I'm sure you can appreciate I didn't want to get off on the wrong foot. We Yanks have a reputation for being so noisy and forward."

I asked about her family.

"Oh, them," she said airily. "Well, I have two brothers, Harrison and Woodrow, but they're too boring. My daddy's a diplomat, so we live close to the US Embassy down in Knightsbridge – don't you just love that name? – and my mother used to be a nurse until she met him. All very romantic. He was so ill with appendicitis, and she looked after him, and well, that was that!"

As we talked over lunch on the first day, she admitted to being 'a bit of a' swimmer.

"Bring a cozzie tomorrow," I said, "and come and swim with us after school."

Like me, Tara's quite tall and slender, but she must have amazing power in those long legs. When we did a few lengths to warm up, she rippled away from us in a perfect, elegant crawl stroke. Mrs Williams often says to me that I make swimming look far too much like hard work, that she can see the effort I'm putting in, and that I must relax more in the water. Tara's style today was a perfect demonstration of what I think she's talking about. She really uses the full stretch of her arms to pull through each stroke. I could see at once what Sarah and I could learn from her.

As we walked back to the tube, she said casually, "Yeah, well, it's just too bad, isn't it, that Daddy got posted to London. The swimming was going really well back home. It's a shame."

"What level were you competing at?" asked Sarah.

"Fifth in the US champs last year," Tara answered.

"What age group was that?" I said, and somehow I knew the answer before she opened her mouth in reply.

"Oh no," Tara said, and she really wasn't boasting or anything, "I mean, the full US championships. The real deal. That's why my mom and daddy sent me to CCS. They'd heard about your Mrs Williams, and thought it'd be the next best thing to the coaching I had in Boston. Because one day we'll go back home, and then maybe I can swim competitively again."

Saturday 21st September 1935

Mrs Williams has now taken to calling us her 'three musketeers', which would be completely cringeworthy if Tara, Sarah and I didn't like each other so much.

The sessions with the Mermaid club went very well over the summer. Sarah and I have been getting gradually stronger and faster under the constant guidance of Mrs Williams' stopwatch which measures our every last moment in the water. And since Sarah has started concentrating on her freestyle and backstroke swimming, she's begun to push me all the way. She's consistently quicker off the mark than I am, and most times has me beaten over 110 yards, but my stamina's still much greater than hers.

"If there was a one-mile race for ladies," Mrs Williams has said more than once, "you'd be a challenger, Eleanor, and no doubt about it. Your shoulders are a great gift. But you lack Sarah's concentration."

I try to look on the comment about the shoulders as a compliment, remembering Father's comments about 'unladylike', 'unbecoming' etc.

Talking about Father, in the end we even fitted in a

summer holiday for the three of us. After that dinner-table conversation I think he felt a little guilty, so a week was taken in the Imperial Hotel in Bournemouth during the middle of August, and very nice it was too. We travelled there and back first class from London, with a cab to take us all the way from Edgware to the excitement of grand, smoky Waterloo Station on the other side of the River Thames. Mother never complains, but I think she finds it a relief to get away from Grandpa from time to time. His solemn, silent presence around Seymour Lodge becomes a bit much after a while.

The weather was kind to us down on the south coast, and while Father read the papers, watched cricket, and played bowls, Mother and I strolled up and down the Prom.

She indulged me while I used the opportunity to swim in open water as much as I could. Many of the major championships are held in open-water baths so it's good to take every chance while it's there. We went to a couple of concerts in the evenings, and a lovely time was had by all.

Earlier this week I plucked up courage and asked could Sarah and Tara come to tea today. We've entertained Sarah on her own before, and I wondered if it was a bit of a nerve to ask if the two of them could come together, but Mother seemed delighted. They arrived soon after lunch, and then, because it was a lovely early autumn day, we caught the tram to Stanmore, and walked up into the woods of the Harrow Weald to see if the leaves were turning yet. There was just a

24

hint of yellow among the greens.

We followed the line of Grimsdyke through the trees, and I told Tara how the ditches and banks had been built by the Saxons to mark their territory a thousand or more years ago. Her eyes widened.

"A thousand years! You see, that's what we Americans find so incredible about England. You guys have all this history lying around and think nothing of it. In Boston, we have a few old buildings and stuff, but nothing like this."

We peeked into the grounds of Grimsdyke House with its gloopy ponds and air of melancholy, even on a sunny day.

"Feels sad, doesn't it?" I said. "My grandpa once knew the man who lived here. He was a famous composer ... well, he was half of a famous musical team ... called W.S. Gilbert."

"I know about him," said Tara, "Gilbert and Sullivan. My mama sang in the chorus for his *Pirates of Penzance* back in Boston!"

"Well, that's where he met a sticky end," I said, pointing at the ponds. "He liked swimming there..."

"With his friends," added Sarah, eyes flashing mischievously. "With no clothes on!"

"Anyway," I said ignoring her. "One day, something went wrong, and he drowned, probably trying to rescue one of them."

It's a very odd thing. Grimsdyke House always has a way of making people feel thoughtful, even if they don't know the story, and although Sarah had been joking and teasing a minute or two before, she was suddenly very quiet as we walked down the hill off the Weald.

"Penny for them?" I said.

"Oh, it's nothing to do with anything really. It's just when you said about W.S. Gilbert trying to rescue someone, it set my mind running. My favourite aunt and uncle – Hanna and Jakob – are having a bad time in Germany. Ever since I was little they've always been very kind, sending me presents and writing letters. It worries me to hear how their life is changing."

"What's so awful about Germany?" asked Tara. "I sometimes hear Daddy muttering about it, but I don't really understand."

"There are new laws," Sarah replied. "Since last weekend, when there was a big rally in the city of Nuremberg, Jews have no rights as citizens any longer. And the dreadful thing for Auntie Hanna and Uncle Jakob is, they've always been so proud to be German. Now they can't even fly the new German flag on their little house in Berlin. When my grandparents decided they would come to England to work in 1900 it caused no end of family trouble, and of course the Great War made everything worse, with half of us on one side and half on the other. For a few years no one talked to anyone else, although they eventually made it up after the war ended. But now Auntie Hanna and Uncle Jakob are saying they don't know what will become of them. They're convinced nasty Mr Hitler will make it harder and harder for Jews to live there. He has some very peculiar ideas about what being a German means. If you aren't tall with blue eyes and fair hair it seems you're not welcome. Some friends of theirs have already been beaten up by Hitler's so-called storm troopers. The brownshirts set about them in broad daylight when they were leaving their house one day. Not one of their neighbours dared to lift a finger."

"So why don't your aunt and uncle just leave and come here?" asked Tara, slightly carelessly, with the air of someone who was used to travelling the world.

"Well for one thing, my uncle used to work for the German civil service until two years ago. Then they fired all the Jews, and he's had no regular job since. He plays the piano in a bar some evenings of the week, and I think my aunt acts as a part-time secretary for some writer, but there's not enough money coming in for them to think about moving. And I don't think they can really believe what's happening to them. Just think, Tara, how you would feel if you knew you could never go back to America."

There was just a hint of reproach in what Sarah said. It was the first remotely awkward moment between the three of us. Clouds flitted across the skies of Sarah's eyes, and for a moment it looked like rain, but then, being Sarah, the sun came out almost the very next moment and there she was, laughing the matter off.

"We're survivors, we Jews," she said, pulling herself together. "Something will turn up. I'm sure Hitler can't really be as bad as he's painted. And he says he's doing these things to protect us anyway. That's why he's banned Jews from marrying outside their religion."

We were in sight of the new housing estates outside Edgware now, and we quickened our steps. Tea and cake were calling. What did Germany matter? Except, I thought to myself, this is the country – the very city – where they're going to hold the Olympic Games. How's that going to work?

And now, writing this, I think about my father, and the tone of voice he uses when he talks about Jews 'flocking to Edgware', and I can't work it out. Is he really so against it, or is he just teasing, the way he does sometimes? I can't remotely understand why anyone would want to be horrible to my lovely friend Sarah and her good, honourable family. It makes no sense to me at all.

Friday 27th September 1935

A very peculiar man came to supper at Seymour Lodge tonight, and I fell out with my father over it. I probably behaved very badly, but I'm going to write down what happened, as Miss Wilson says, so that perhaps I'll understand myself a bit better.

His name is Sir Oswald Mosley, and to look at, he's what my father would call 'a fine figure of a man'. He's tall and well-built and his black, brilliantined hair sweeps back dramatically across his head. He has equally finely manicured dark eyebrows and a pencil moustache. His left eyebrow is very odd, because when he wants to, he can raise it effortlessly, without the other one moving in the least. He obviously does it as a sort of trick to impress people. He walks with a limp which is the result of a wound from the Great War, or so Mother told me, although he must have been very young when he received it. He was dressed very smartly, although in so much black he reminded me rather of an undertaker (I said this quietly to Mother just after Sir Oswald walked in through the front door, and she nearly had hysterics!). Tonight he brought with him a lady called Lady Diana Mitford, who I thought was very beautiful, but also very distant and cold. She gave the impression that the whole evening was a chore, and that it was all a bit beneath her. As I suppose it was, really. She's obviously frightfully upper-class.

Mother was all of a flap. Both Amy and Mrs Etheridge had been summoned to cook and serve dinner. It turned out that my father had helped Sir Oswald when he'd stood for Parliament in the Harrow constituency some years ago, but

29

I haven't got to the bottom of why he and his 'friend' were dining with us tonight. Did Father invite them? Or did they invite themselves? Or as Grandpa would say, "Who's buying and who's selling?"

I was instructed to put on my best dress, brush my hair, and be politely present at dinner. There was small talk at first, and I suppose Sir Oswald was trying to be nice to me. He said he had a daughter of his own, but that he didn't see her as often as he'd like. He asked me about school and my friends. I mentioned Sarah and Tara, but when I said the name Sarah Rosenthal, I was sure I noticed a little curl of the lip. At first I assumed I was just being over-sensitive after my conversation with Sarah the other day, but later on over the pudding course (choice of two, so it was clearly an important evening), things took a turn for the worse. The subject was – inevitably – how Edgware was changing.

"We came back here," my father said, between first and second helpings of trinity pudding (with a compôte of last year's prize plums!), "so that there'd be a bit more room to move, if you know what I mean. And then, lo and behold what do we find? Five years later it's a come-all-ye, and the place is filling up with every sort."

There was a general harrumphing and agreement that this was all too bad.

"A lot of new money, I suppose?" said Mosley.

"By the looks of it, yes," replied my father. "And too often wasted on vulgar taste."

"A Jewish element?"

"I should say so. Even a synagogue down on Station Road, right in the middle of town. Makes us feel very uncomfortable over at St. Margaret's, I must say."

The words 'Jewish element' put my back up straight away. And at this point the haughty Lady Diana Mitford, who until then had been pretty silent, said in hushed tones, "I had the incredible privilege of being in Nuremberg last week to listen to Herr Hitler. He's a truly great man, you know, a man of destiny. It was all utterly marvellous. I believe they're making a film of the proceedings, so very soon everyone will be able to see how wonderful things are there. Herr Hitler and his colleagues are taking steps, as I'm sure you've heard, Mr Rhys Davies, in respect of the Jewish problem. If Sir Oswald were our leader here, and with the help of men like you, surely we could follow their example, and neutralize the Jewish danger to our British way of life?"

I stared at her hard, but she wouldn't meet my gaze. She has very funny eyes, that woman.

"The Jewish money, Rhys Davies. That's the problem," continued Mosley. "It floods the market, and weakens the moral fibre of the British economy and state. Time's short. You've seen it here on your doorstep, and you must know it through the information which comes to you in Whitehall. We have to act before it's too late. We should value a man in

31

your position coming to join us. There's a place ready and waiting for you, you can be sure of that."

There was more of this long-winded kind of stuff, which I can't now remember. Sir Oswald's words were swimming around inside my brain, bumping into each other. I couldn't believe that my father would seriously consider having anything to do with this odious man. I felt light-headed. I knew I had to say something.

"My friend Sarah..." I at last piped up, and it was nice to see Sir Oswald very nearly drop his fork in surprise. He clearly expected little girls to be seen and not heard. My voice sounded very small and clear in the dining room. "My friend Sarah has an aunt and uncle in Germany who have lost their jobs because they are Jewish, consequently have no money because they are Jewish, cannot vote or fly a German flag because they are Jewish, and are in fear of their lives because they are Jewish. Do you really think that can be right, Sir Oswald? With all respect, sir, would that be a British way of doing things?"

There was a deathly silence. My mother looked down at her plate, her expression saying something like 'That's torn it!' My father's face was like thunder. He chewed a non-existent mouthful for a moment and then spoke.

"If I or Sir Oswald had wanted your opinion, we should have asked for it, Eleanor. I think you should leave us now. I do apologize for my daughter's behaviour, Sir Oswald."

I picked up my napkin, squashed it and placed it on my plate. Then I slowly drew back my chair, and with as much dignity as I could muster, left the dining room to go upstairs. And only once I was safely inside my bedroom and lying on my bed, did I cry noiseless, sobbing tears into my pillow. What had I done?

It was fifteen minutes or so before my mother came up.

"Oh darling," she said, stroking my heaving back. "I don't think you should have said that."

"What I said was right," I insisted, turning to face her. "Wasn't it? How can speaking the truth be wrong?"

She said nothing but just kept stroking my hair. I took her silence for secret agreement. But how will I make it up with Father?

Saturday 28th September 1935

I didn't sleep very well last night for thinking about what had happened. At breakfast, seeing my red and bleary eyes, and knowing I wouldn't be able to bear Father's bad opinion of me, Mother told me he'd gone into work for the morning – which at a weekend is very unusual even for him. He returned just after lunch, and sent a message via a nervous-looking Amy at about three o'clock to say he wanted to see me in his study. I knocked at the door, and he opened it, still smartly dressed for work. On Saturday afternoons he usually wears an open-necked shirt with a sports jacket.

"Come in, Ellie," he said, and the moment he used my shortened name I knew he wasn't still angry with me. He motioned to me to sit down, and then moved his chair to sit beside rather than opposite me. He examined his fingernails for a while, apparently searching for the right words. I shivered as I waited. His study always strikes me as a cold place.

"I learned two things last evening," he said eventually. "The first is how quickly you're growing up. When you have children of your own you may find you one day have the same experience. You look away for an instant, and when you turn back … the person looks and sounds different. While you haven't been paying attention, just as if you were Rip van Winkle and had been asleep for years, there's been a change. I remember it being so when you stopped being a baby, and suddenly became a child. And now all of a sudden you're a young woman..."

He paused.

"And the second thing, which I say with more hesitation, is that I think you and I are quite alike. We sometimes speak before we think, which is sometimes a good idea and sometimes not. I've never quite rid myself of the habit, so I can't entirely blame you for inheriting the fault – if fault it is. I can't even say you were impolite last evening, because you weren't. What you said was inconvenient, no more. True, but inconvenient."

I tried to stick my oar in at this point to say I was sorry, but he held up his hand to prevent me.

"On the other hand, what you have yet to learn is that life is never simple or one-sided, and sometimes things aren't entirely what they seem. Sometimes I will say things in your company that I'm trying on for size – as you may do with me. I think we're entitled to that in our own house, don't you? We may not completely believe everything we say, but it's better we test things out here in the safety of Seymour Lodge than make fools of ourselves in public. That's all I wanted to say to you, Ellie, and I'll say no more now, but leave you to think about what I've said."

And that was it.

The more I do think about it, the more puzzled I am. Does he also secretly agree with me? And what are the things I've heard him say and thought he meant, which he was really 'only trying on for size'? And if he doesn't like Sir Oswald Mosley, why did he have him and the Mitford person to dinner?

Wednesday 16th October 1935

The nights are drawing in now, which is jolly bad news all round, I should say. For a start, whereas Father might turn a blind eye to his one and only beloved daughter traipsing around London in the long, light summer evenings, now it's dark so early he wants me home and safe from the terrors and disgrace that lie waiting for a young girl in the winter shadows. And it's also the end of the swimming season. No more races and competitions, just the hard work of training without the carrot of cups, medals and certificates to be won. Roll on spring!

Last night there was a whizzy last hurrah for the season at the Marshall Street Baths which are slap bang in the middle of London near Regent Street. Thanks to Mrs Williams, we three Camden lasses got a special dispensation from Miss Bowes to be allowed out till midnight so that we could swim. The condition was that we were back at school on time this morning, bright-eyed and bushy-tailed, which we just about managed despite Mother asking "Are you sure you'll be all right, dear?" about half a dozen times over breakfast. However, as I shall explain, the evening produced just the teeniest cloud on the blue horizon.

The occasion was a Grand International Swimming Gala to raise funds for the Mermaid Swimming Club. The club wanted to hold it in the West End to give things a sense of importance and so that all the VIPs didn't have to trudge up to Hampstead, which some people seem to think is the end of the earth. It was going to be an awful lot of fun, Mrs Williams said, with the emphasis on female swimmers for a change, and so it was. There were diving exhibitions, a water polo match, one-on-one races between top swimmers old and new, comedy swimming, life-saving, relay races, even a brass band treading water furiously, and somewhere in the middle of the programme our little spot. All Mrs Williams had said was that she'd arranged for the three of us Camden girls to line up over 220 yards freestyle against three other good young swimmers from around London, including Margaret Jeffrey, the girl who beat me at Hastings. But then, so she should, because Mrs Williams says Margaret's nailed on to make the international team next year. Anyway when I arrived at the pool with Mother, and she bought a sixpenny programme on the door, what did we see halfway down the second page but: '9.15: London's water babes show us what they're made of...'

'Water babes'! That would be us then.

"Oh dear," said my mother. "I hope your father never gets to see this. Whatever was Mrs Williams thinking about! As

37

for showing the world what you're made of, I think that's exactly what concerns him."

At which point Mrs Williams hove into view, covered in confusion and explaining that really she'd no idea, and was most dreadfully sorry. Heads would roll back in Hampstead over this one.

"I shouldn't imagine Miss Bowes will be too amused either," said Mother tartly. Mrs Williams obviously hadn't thought of that until now. Her eyes rolled up into her head in anguish and her face went an even deeper shade of pink.

"Well anyway," she said, "let's get changed, shall we, Eleanor?"

The race itself went absolutely spiffingly. It was the first time the three of us had raced against each other in public, and though we were all our normal nice selves about it, it still sort of mattered who won. Although I say it myself, I swam out of my skin. I knew there was nothing in it until we turned for the final length, but then I felt a surge of energy as I set off for home. Somehow I knew that this would be my night. I stretched to touch in a fraction before Tara in the next lane, and as I bounced up from the water I saw that Sarah was some way behind. She hadn't been feeling very well – the race had come just at the wrong time for her – and I wasn't surprised that she was a bit off the pace. Twisting around I could see Margaret Jeffrey to Tara's right, shaking her head in disappointment.

"Where did she come? Where did she come?" I screamed at Tara over the racket from the cheering crowd.

"I dunno," said Tara. "But she's not a happy bunny."

Apparently, Margaret had caught her hand and wrist in the cork lane markers a couple of times, and had almost stopped at one point in the middle of the race. And true, 220 isn't her best distance. But no matter, I (and Tara) had beaten a prospective Olympic competitor. The time must have been good too: Mrs Williams was jumping up and down on the pool side, waving her stopwatch.

"Two fifty-two and a bit for you, young Eleanor. And two fifty two and a bit more for you, Tara. Terrific stuff. Well done!"

At least by doing so well we've probably saved her bacon. A triumph for the 'Camden water babes'. Let's hope neither Miss Bowes or darling Father asks to see the programme.

Friday 18th October 1935

All hope is gone, and our identity revealed. Apparently it was all in a Hampstead local newspaper, the *Ham and High*. 'Mermaid SC Water Babes Triumph in West End Swim Dash'. And just in case anyone was uncertain who we might be, there was a picture of Tara and me getting our medals and looking much too delighted with ourselves. I know this because Joyce Phillips was waving a copy all round the form-room today at Camden. She thought we'd be pleased. Question. Where does Miss Bowes live? And does my father ever read the local papers?

Sunday 27th October 1935

CCS is more than fifty years old, which is easy to believe as you tread daintily along its stone and wood-panelled corridors and staircases. But the school has always believed in 'doing good for others less fortunate than ourselves'. And since one is now in the Upper Fifth form and therefore very nearly a 'senior girl', there's no escape from taking a full part in the 'do-gooding' whether one likes it or not. (Or whether those on the receiving end like it or not?)

Some years ago (sorry about the history lesson but this won't make sense unless you know why Sarah and I ended up in the wrong part of London on a Saturday afternoon in half-term), the school bought an old church hall in Hackney, where a lot of the 'less fortunate' live, and spruced it up to be what they call a community centre. Now there are weekly meetings for old people, a Women's Bright Hour on Wednesday afternoons, a Sunday school, and lots of other things like that, run by the citizens of Hackney with CCS money. And at some point all of us girls are roped in to help, with a definite black mark if you dare to look as if you'd rather not. Yesterday was the annual school-run Jumble Sale, which had sounded much more fun than looking after a crèche (Yuck! Nappies! Double-yuck!) or making polite conversation with Hackney hobbledehoys, so back in September I volunteered promptly and stuck Sarah's hand up in the air too so that there'd be some good company.

For weeks piles of old tat have been arriving at the school. Because a lot of CCS families are too rich or too proud for hand-me-downs (and in my case there's no one to hand-me-down to!) old clothes have to go somewhere, and in Camden this is where they go. On Friday a van came to take the jumble across London, and our task was to turn up at Hazeldene Hall in Hackney at ten o'clock sharp to help finish the sorting so that the Grand Sale could open its doors at two.

"I'm sort of excited," said Sarah as the Circle Line carriages rumbled round towards the Bank station where we had to change trains. "Why is that?"

"Me too," I replied. "I think it just means that we lead pathetically dull and boring lives, compared with the characters in Rose Gershwin's books, so anything the least bit out of the ordinary counts as exciting. Still, it's a bit off the beaten track. And that's always interesting, isn't it?"

I'm going to sound snobby, but East London feels very different from where we live now, or even Islington – where we used to live. The buildings all seem closer together and a bit grubbier. And the people speak more roughly and quickly, to the point that although I'm a Londoner through and through, I sometimes can't make out what they're saying. They look different too, I'm sure of it, somehow swarthier and more thin-faced.

"Do you think we're safe? I'm not sure I like being here all that much," I remarked as we walked from Bromley-by-Bow tube.

"Don't you?" said Sarah. "I do. You'll see. It's got more life about it than boring old Edgware. It's rather like being in a Dickens novel. You never know what you're going to see next."

"Well, let's hope there aren't too many thieves and pickpockets," I said half-jokingly.

"There wouldn't be much point in picking my pocket," she laughed.

Jolly Miss Abrahams was waiting for us alongside other adult helpers in a very chilly Hazeldene Hall, surrounded by trestle tables and boxes.

"Ooh, I'm very glad to see you two," she said, waving her hands at a mountain of sundry garments. "We've got our work cut out with all these clothes."

We sorted while she priced up the various items for sale. There was the very good and the very bad. It's amazing what some people will throw out, and equally amazing what other people think is fit to pass on. There were some lovely smart dresses that had scarcely been worn, and one gentleman's dress suit which might have had the occasional outing to the Ritz or the theatre, but was still completely immaculate.

"Perhaps it was the wrong size..." I wondered aloud.

"Or maybe he just died..." Sarah chipped in.

"Ugh," I said, dropping the jacket as if it were a hot potato. "Sarah!"

On the other hand there were some things that were so disgusting I was glad I was wearing gloves: sweaty old liberty bodices, grey with age, food-encrusted shirts, holed shoes, and even a gruesomely blood-stained pair of trousers.

"I wonder what the story is behind these?" I said holding them up to the light.

"I dread to think," said Sarah wrinkling her nose. "Murder? A road accident? Who knows..."

"In the bin!" said Miss Abrahams firmly. "Goodness, it makes you realise how the other half lives, doesn't it!"

By half past one, there was a queue of customers halfway down the street, and when the hall doors were pulled back on the dot of two, a scrum of desperate East Enders fought their way into the room, pushing and plundering their way towards whatever bargains they thought they could see.

43

Elbows were being freely dug into ribs, and knees and toes into thighs and ankles. When the first rush was over, Miss Abrahams wiped her brow and gave us the nod that they could cope now. We were free to go.

"Well, that was an experience!" said Sarah, as we walked off back towards the tube station. "But I wouldn't have missed it for the world. Did you see the large woman with the umbrella and the bunch of pretend cherries on her hat. I wouldn't like to meet her on a dark night. She wasn't taking any prisoners."

"I can't really believe it," I said, slightly stunned. "I know they said there are poor people living round here, but the look in some of those eyes ... frightening!"

We nattered on, as we do, when suddenly it occurred to me that the street we were in looked unfamiliar.

"Have we missed our way?" I asked.

"Don't think so," Sarah answered. "It's down here and turn left, isn't it?"

Puzzled, I said I thought we needed to turn right, if anything.

"No, no, I'm sure it's left," Sarah insisted, and she seemed so certain, we did as she suggested.

After a hundred yards or so, we began to hear the sound of people shouting and yelling up ahead.

"Is there a football match being played near here this afternoon?" Sarah asked. "West Ham, maybe?"

"How would I know?" I snorted, and checked my watch.

It was half past three. "Anyway, even if there was, they'd all be inside the ground now – they'd be halfway through the match."

As we came up towards a main road where there was a long parade of little shops, the shouting came into focus. It was distinctly unfriendly, and suddenly there was the sound of breaking glass, accompanied by a roar of anger from what sounded like a sizeable crowd. We stopped and looked at each other.

"Shall we go back the way we came?" I said.

"Don't you want to see what the fuss is all about?"

I could see Sarah's point. It seemed a bit lame just to creep away, and never know.

"All right then," I conceded. "Just a quick look."

We almost tiptoed up to the corner, which was completely daft, since a herd of fairy elephants charging along with us wouldn't have raised an eyebrow just then. Two groups of men were facing each other along the centre of the road. One group seemed to be a bunch of ordinary working people, in caps and overalls. The other was swankily dressed all in black, and carried placards. Some of them simply had the initials BUF on them in large letters. Other placards read: 'We will walk where we want', or 'British workers for British jobs'. And very clearly at least one just said 'Jewish scum'.

I was horrified. I hoped that Sarah hadn't seen that. But as I glanced round at her, I could see she had. Her face had drained of all its colour, and over the noise and confusion, I heard her shout, "It's the British Union of Fascists. Mosley's poisonous lot."

And sure enough, towards the back of the black-shirted mob could be seen the limping figure of Sir Oswald Mosley, chest puffed out, head held high, flanked by a little knot of muscle-men. As they passed on up the street, the two groups of men jostled each other, insults were traded and the odd punch was thrown. We shrank back into a doorway and watched as the Fascists passed on up the street, and the Jewish shopkeepers waved fists and sticks at their departing backs.

"Where are the police?" said Sarah. "Why isn't anyone helping these men protect their shops? And what about the synagogue?"

"What synagogue?"

"There's a synagogue near here."

"How do you know?"

"We go there for Rosh Hashanah."

"But we're lost..."

"Not all that lost!"

"So where's Bromley-by-Bow station?"

"I don't know. We'll have to ask."

Sarah wasn't making much sense, but in the circumstances I wasn't going to argue. We stopped an old woman who was walking towards us, tutting and shaking her head in annoyance. She looked at us suspiciously. She could see I at least didn't belong there.

"You're way out, ducks," she said, directing her words to Sarah. "You wants Mile End tube now if you're going up west. Half a mile that way."

She pointed up the main road in the opposite direction from the Fascist march. We thanked her and set off.

Sarah was grim-faced as we walked.

"To tell or not to tell?" I asked.

"Not to tell," Sarah said firmly. "After all, what good would it do? You and I can't stop the Fascists. Only the government can do that. What parents don't know, they won't grieve over."

Remembering what she'd said on the way to the jumble sale, I tried a little humour.

"More life than jolly old Edgware then," I said and grinned hopefully.

"Interesting," she replied with a deadpan expression. "And instructive. But only exciting if you're a certain sort of person, I should imagine."

Friday 8th November 1935

It's ten o'clock in the evening as I write this, and I know it's after 'lights out', but I just don't care. I'm feeling very sorry for myself, and I don't mind telling you I've had a little weep about it all. Life is so unfair.

For a start I've had a miserable cold for about ten days now, and it's been difficult enough dragging myself out of the house and off to school as it is.

"Goodness Ellie, you look like death warmed up," was what Sarah said as soon as she saw me at the station on Monday morning. "Go home. You should be in bed." Well, if it's obvious to my friends, why are the teachers so stupid? But perhaps she just didn't want to catch what I'd got.

The second thing is, we had the results back from our half-term tests on Tuesday. In every other year the tests only come at the end of each term, but in the Upper Fifth they test us twice in the autumn term and then leave us alone until the General Exams in June, which we have to pass to get into the Sixth Form. Or not. Anyway, at registration there were the results, pinned up on the form-room notice board for everyone to read. I looked and looked and couldn't quite believe what I saw. My ears started burning, and I had that awful tickly hot feeling in my neck that I used to get when I was little and had been caught doing something naughty. The only half-decent marks I'd managed were in English and history. In all the other subjects I was way, way down the class, even in French – which everyone knows I'm really good at. I won't tell you what I got for maths, except I was third from bottom, just above Jean Findlay who's as thick as two short planks. Really. She'll even tell you that herself.

So I was already in trouble, and after that things went from bad to completely horrible. After morning break on Tuesdays we have chemistry. Miss Halliwell the chemistry teacher isn't my favourite person. She's the worst sort because she'll come down on you like a ton of bricks for the least thing, but she's obviously bone idle. She can never be bothered to mark work thoroughly, and if she's decided you're unlikely to be a star at science – which I'm probably not – she hasn't got the patience to explain things properly.

As you face the blackboard in the chemistry lab there are two fume cabinets to your left at the front and back, and between them is an open fire without which the lab would be very cold in winter, because it's right at the top of the CCS building and there are lots of glass skylights which let out all the warmth. The colder it gets the more Miss Halliwell likes to sit on a high stool by the fire, hogging as much of the heat as she can while we shiver. It being a chem. lab there are always horrible smells hanging around, but on Tuesday there was suddenly an extra nasty niff which penetrated even my blocked sinuses. Miss Halliwell seemed completely oblivious, but when she finally moved her bottom off the stool to wobble up to the blackboard, we could see that a considerable portion of the back of her skirt had gone up in smoke. Understandably a number of us found this immensely humorous. Unfortunately when she rounded on us in a temper, it was me she saw holding my sides and gasping for breath. So that was one 'signature' in the great CCS book of sins and offences.

A second was rapidly added on Wednesday in the course of my annual interview and medical inspection with Bagshaw, the school nurse. For some reason she's never liked me. I have to say the feeling's entirely mutual. She's a silly old bat.

"You're too thin," she announced, as I stood in front of her in bra and knickers clasping my shoulders to keep warm. "You're obviously not eating enough."

"I don't think my mother would agree," I said.

"Mothers rarely know best," she harrumphed. "And daughters hide the truth. Look at you. No colour in the face, except for those red eyes. She obviously lets you stay up too late, listening to the radio or some such."

"She doesn't," I argued. "She's very strict about bedtimes. And I've had a bad cold for a week."

"Rubbish," went Bagshaw. "It's just a question of mind over matter. The last cold I had was ten years ago, during the General Strike. I should imagine you pick up infections all the time because you swim too much. What do you expect from using Public Baths?" She spoke the last two words as if she was dealing with something unmentionable.

"Do you swim, Miss Bagshaw?" I asked hotly. "Because if you did you'd know that these days the water's chlorinated to the point that every self-respecting germ packs its bags and leaves town rather than waste its time on us. And I do not swim too much. I swim because it's healthy and fun, and actually, I'm rather good. Ask Mrs Williams."

I won't bore you with the way the conversation went on from there. You can imagine. Enough to say the words 'How dare you...' cropped up a couple of times and 'Insolence' and 'Answering back' got honourable mentions. It also became apparent that she knew how bad my test results had been. So that was 'signature' number two.

The rules are: three 'signatures' in a half-term and you're up before Miss Bowes. This is no laughing matter, and doesn't happen very often. It's never happened to me, for all that Miss Bowes and I have had the occasional discussion about the meaning of life. Three 'signatures' in three days is more or less unheard of, but yes, somehow I managed it. Why exactly Miss Byron, the other PE teacher, took it into her head that I was the person ideally suited to fill the vacant space in the under-sixteen hockey team to play the Henrietta Barnet School this afternoon I don't know. I don't like hockey. I'm not very good at hockey. And I'm ill. I told her so. But perhaps I didn't tell her so in the right way, I'll admit that much.

Justice is administered promptly at CCS, which I suppose is a good thing, rather than having the prospect of humiliation hang over you for days.

"It's not been your best week, has it?" Miss Bowes suggested, as I sat wretchedly in front of her, sniffing. I wanted to explain, and justify myself, and say how completely mystified I was that I'd done so badly in the tests. Except I knew the answer to that one. I hadn't revised enough, I really hadn't, and I'd been found out. Of course, it's not a mistake I intend to repeat, but it may be too late. By a combination of bad luck and stupidity it's possible I've spoiled the thing that makes my life worth living.

"I'll be honest with you, Eleanor," she went on. "You're a young woman with considerable talents. But a lot of that talent is going to waste presently. What concerns me is that you're being distracted from the important things of life by trivia. And sadly, along with a liking for a certain sort of cheap literature (how did she know about that?), I must include in that category your very real ability as a swimmer. I fear I must tell your parents that this is so. Your mind is not on your work. And the work, not your athletic prowess, is the reason you have the privilege of attending Camden Collegiate School. If you continue to combine poor academic performance with insubordination, then I fear this is not the place for you."

So now you see why I've been having a little weep.

Thursday 14th November 1935

The letter from Miss Bowes arrived at Seymour Lodge this morning in the first post. It sat on the dinner table all through supper staring at us evilly, and when the dishes had been cleared, Father reached out his hand and carefully slid the two pages of neat typescript from the CCS-crested envelope so that they lay open to view. He was very calm. Mother looked agitated.

"What have you got to say about this, Eleanor?" he asked quietly.

Knowing such a moment might arrive, I'd been preparing a little speech over the last six days which I now more or less had off by heart. I told them I was so sorry I hadn't revised, and that I truly believed I'd learned my lesson. I explained my side of the Bagshaw incident in some detail. Mother furrowed her brow when she heard what the dreadful woman had said about her. I was suitably contrite about Miss Halliwell, and slightly less so about the hockey match. My main argument I left to last.

"The thing is," I said, "if God forbid I'd been born a boy, and you'd sent me to Harrow School, and let's say I'd been brilliant at cricket or rugger, and people said I might play for England one day, do you think the school would turn round and suggest that I just give it all up because I temporarily wasn't doing so well at my school work? You sent me to CCS because you thought it would give me as good an education as any boy could get, so surely that should include the swimming? Why can't they see it will add to the school's reputation if Sarah, Tara and I do well? I agree there's a problem with the number of swimming competitions and galas. We could be off competing every day between April and October, if they let us, and that would be bad and perhaps lead to us getting big-headed, but Mrs Williams has been very careful to limit how much we've done."

Mother seemed to be nodding in agreement. Father's face was impossible to read.

And then, as if it was a rabbit from a magician's hat, Father suddenly produced a copy of the *Ham and High* from his attaché case, folded open at the page with the 'Water babes' headline and the picture of Tara and me. My heart sank. I blushed. He placed it carefully on the table, smoothing the paper flat, and studied it carefully for a moment, turning it around so that Mother could see it in its full glory. She sighed, and ran a tired hand across her face as she sank back in her chair. She and I exchanged guilty glances. Father looked darkly at me, and then at her. "Oh dear," I thought. "Whatever's coming next?" And then his face creased and he almost seemed to giggle in a most un-Father-like way before recovering himself.

"What's frustrating," he began, "is that in one respect Miss Bowes is quite right. You have enormous talents, Ellie, not the least of which is to put together a very convincing argument when you want to. I wish my office juniors had half your gumption. You'd be very good in court. Basically, I agree with you. It's another reason why Sir Oswald Mosley is so wrong. People like him think that men should rule the roost, and women should stay at home to cook meals and have babies, because that's biologically all their minds and bodies are fit for. But living as I do with two such strong-minded women, how could I possibly share that opinion? So. I'll do what you cannot, and argue the point with Miss Bowes, who as far as I can see is herself no shrinking violet. And I will make myself clear about this Bagshaw woman. But..."

I knew there would be a 'but'.

"You must solemnly promise to do your very best with all your school work from now on. No half measures. Be as ruthless as you would be in the pool and always, but always, aim for the highest. Do you promise?"

"I promise."

"Do you solemnly promise?"

"I solemnly promise."

"Very well then. Your father can thus cherish the hope that you become not only a 'water babe', but also a 'chemistry babe', and perhaps even a 'maths babe' too."

"You don't mind too much about ... that?" my mother asked him, fluttering a hand towards the *Ham and High*.

"She looks perfectly decent to me," said my father. "In fact all I see is our darling little girl becoming the attractive, personable, clever young woman we always hoped for. I'm sure she'll turn many heads before she's done."

Wednesday 20th November 1935

As we were going down to assembly at the end of registration this morning, Miss Scaldwell took me on one side and slipped an envelope into my hand.

"For your eyes only," she said, mysteriously.

It was addressed to 'Miss Eleanor Rhys-Davies' in a beautiful handwriting I didn't recognize, the kind I should like to have, but don't at all. I slipped the envelope into my bag, and waited to open it until Sarah and I were together at morning break.

"Well?" said Sarah, as I stared at its contents. On the paper inside was written a single line of Latin, and underneath it the initials 'EB'. It read: '*Igitur natamus ad gloriam omnibus*'.

"You're better at this than me," I said, and gave it to her. My brain goes blank when I first look at a Latin sentence. I thought I knew what it meant but wasn't sure.

"Well, it's definitely 'Therefore we will swim to glory'," said Sarah. "But the 'omnibus' could mean 'in all things' or 'for everyone', I suppose."

"Or perhaps it's meant to be both – like a pun?" I wondered aloud.

"Ellie, you do know who this is from, don't you?" Sarah asked, wide-eyed. "What's Miss Bowes doing writing to you?"

"Yes," I said smiling, "It's not a note at all, really. More a well-disguised olive branch."

Friday 22nd November 1935

Mother looked completely distracted at breakfast. She couldn't sit still, and was thoroughly and unreasonably irritable with Amy about the hardness of the eggs and the strength of the tea – very unusual for her.

"Is anything the matter?" I asked eventually, as she drummed her fingers and fussed with the cutlery.

"It's nothing," she said, the way people do when it's definitely something. "Nothing at all. I'm just being silly. Only … only your father's had to go away on business overnight, and won't be back till late tomorrow."

"So..." This happens occasionally, maybe three or four times a year.

"Oh … I suppose there's no harm in your knowing. But please don't say anything to anyone else, Ellie. They're flying him out from Heston airfield to Germany, and I know I shouldn't worry, but I'm frantic the plane is going to crash."

I must have looked dumbfounded. This had never happened before.

"There," she went on, "I should never have told you, and your father said I shouldn't. Now all I've done is to worry you too."

"Of course you haven't," I said, fibbing just a tiny bit. "Lots of people fly these days. It's all the rage. Where's he going? And who with? And who's he going to see?"

"Well, the aircraft will take them to Cologne. And I know there are a dozen or so in the delegation and that some of them are senior politicians. But I haven't a clue who they're going to see or why. I should imagine it's all rather hush-hush."

"What exactly does Father do?" I ventured. "He never really talks about it."

"I'm learning not to ask," she said. "Perhaps it's better not to know. The world seems a lot more complicated than when we were first married."

She looked a bit wistful. But there wasn't much I could do, or I'd have missed my train.

Saturday 23rd November 1935

Thank goodness for that. Father's back safe and sound as if nothing at all untoward had happened. I wondered about asking him where he'd been, and then thought better of it. But I am simply dying to know.

On a completely different subject, Tara's invited Sarah and me to what she calls 'a sleep-over' this Friday. Apparently there's a children's party at the American Embassy on Saturday afternoon for 'Thanksgiving', whatever that is, and then to make up for having to help with the party, we get treated to a slap-up tea with Tara's parents before we come home. What fun! I thought Father wouldn't allow it, but he was in such a good mood this evening, he'd have said yes to anything, "As long as the homework gets done, Ellie."

Of course it will. The three of us girls can knock it off together on Friday evening.

Monday 2nd December 1935

What a weekend – I don't know where to start. The Macdonalds have a super house in Cavendish Street – not far from Regent Street and the Marshall Street Baths. All very posh at its front with a portico in white plaster set off by black iron railings. Our house is comfortable, but all our furniture is very well 'lived in', if you know what I mean. Inside Tara's house everything is right up to the minute and so smart and fashionable. Both Tara's mother and father are very nice, but I couldn't get over the fact that Tara calls her father 'sir' all the time. I think it's just what they do in America to be polite.

"Do you think we should too?" I asked Sarah on the QT.

She shrugged her shoulders. "Not a clue. But you know what they say ... 'When in Rome...'"

We three had a riotous, giggly girls' time on Friday evening and Saturday morning. And yes, we got the homework done too, although our maths answers may now all look suspiciously similar.

The party at the Embassy was a tiny bit gruesome from the point of view of having to take five-year-olds off to the loo every other minute, but we were driven there in an absolutely huge American car – I mean 'automobile'! We three sat in the back together, and there was still room for more. The Embassy was very grand, though we didn't see a lot of it apart from the ballroom. There was a clown, and a fire-eater, and a projector set up with a screen so that the children could watch some Charlie Chaplin films. And bad news, we had to organize them into playing musical chairs, and those silly games where you have to pass an apple around just using your neck and chin, which is just a quick way of spreading germs if you ask me. Anyone for the measles? The children seemed to be from other foreign embassies in London, so some of them didn't even speak English, which was quite amusing. Where sign language didn't work, we ended up pushing them from place to place to keep the games going. Whether they all understood what was going on I'm not sure, but they didn't seem to mind too much. After they'd been fed, and packed off home, the Embassy staff took over for the cleaning and tidying up while we drove back in Mr Macdonald's Packard to Cavendish Street.

What Tara had called 'tea' in her invitation didn't at all do justice to what actually followed. It was more or less an early Christmas lunch complete with turkey and all the trimmings. Apparently this is strictly speaking what you should do on the last Thursday of November for Thanksgiving in America, to say thank you because the harvest is safe and sound in the barns – which is why there's corn and pumpkin and so on in the meal, and also (which I suppose I wasn't quite so sure of), to say thank you because they think America is the best country in the world. At least, that's the way it came across, though with Mr Macdonald you can never be quite sure if he's teasing. In some ways, he's spookily like my own father, just with a different accent.

"Mr Roosevelt, the President, thinks we should celebrate Thanksgiving a week earlier," said Mr Macdonald.

Everyone looked surprised, including Tara and her brothers.

"He thinks it'd be better for the shops and the economy if there were a longer gap between Thanksgiving and Christmas, so that folks will spend more," he continued between mouthfuls of pumpkin pie. "But I'm not so sure the American people will wear it. Old habits die hard, and they like their Thanksgiving just fine where it is. So tell me, Ellie and Sarah, how's the swimming going? I hear you're cutting Tara down to size."

We made polite noises about how good Tara was, and what fun it was to have someone new to keep us company.

"Tara reckons you might make the British team for the Olympic Games," he went on. "Now, you look like intelligent young women to me. So tell me, do you think it's OK to give Mr Hitler the free publicity of holding the Games in Berlin when he's being quite such a pain in the ass?"

He was looking straight at me when he said this. I nearly choked, and reached for a glass of water.

"Randolph!" said Mrs Macdonald.

"It's OK, Beatrice. They're all right. From what I remember of my school days, they'll have heard plenty worse. So what do you think, girls? Should the governments of Britain and the US threaten to take our ball home, if Hitler doesn't behave himself?"

My mind had gone a complete blank, but luckily Sarah hadn't lost her tongue.

"I have relations living near Berlin," she said. "And they are having a bad time. But maybe if more people from England and America could see what Herr Hitler's doing to them, it would make him stop."

"Well, I'm sorry to hear about your folks. But do you think the good people of Europe and America will ever get to see what's happening?" Mr Macdonald asked more gently. "The Nazis have it sewn up tighter than a Thanksgiving turkey. Hitler employs a man called Joseph Goebbels to mastermind a propaganda war. His job is to make sure Germany looks the best place you could ever imagine living. If the athletes do go to Berlin, the cameras won't catch a hair out of place, you mark my words. Which is why I have to tell you there may not be any American swimmers or runners in Berlin next summer, or any American skaters and skiers at Garmisch-Partenkirchen for the Winter Olympics either. A decision will have to be made very soon. The Winter Games are only a couple of months away, you know."

I wanted to argue back, and say I didn't think cutting Germany off from the rest of the world would do much good, but my courage deserted me. Mr Macdonald can be quite a fearsome man.

I thought I looked like the village idiot pretty much all the way through the meal, but I can't have been too hopeless because as Tara walked us to the tube later on she said (rather tactlessly, I thought), "Well, you were a big hit with Harrison, Ellie! He thinks you're very smart."

Harrison is her seventeen-year-old brother. Woodrow is only thirteen or so. They'd both been very reserved all weekend, so it was difficult to get much impression of them beyond their neat haircuts. They also seemed permanently welded into collars and ties, except at tea, when the neckties were swapped for tartan bow ties which slightly gave Sarah and me an attack of the hysterics.

"Was I?" I said, "Gosh. Well. How nice."

Boys and what they get up to seem to concern Tara much more than they do me. She sometimes talks about Edward, who she says was her 'boyfriend' back in Boston. She still writes to him, which is quite sweet, but honestly what would you want a boyfriend for? One day perhaps, but not yet. There's far too much to do. And Father would have a fit. Let alone Miss Bowes.

Sunday 8th December 1935

We're having a break from training until the New Year, so all this last week, in every spare minute, I have revised my socks off for the mock exams which begin tomorrow. I know *Julius Caesar* and *Pride and Prejudice* inside out and back to front, I can tell you anything you want to know about the Corn Laws, I almost know what to do with the French subjunctive, and thanks to Sarah's patient explanation my algebra isn't quite as hopeless as it was. I have honestly done my best. But will it be good enough? I won't know until we come back next term.

Tuesday 24th December 1935

First of two Christmas treats. Last night Father and Mother took us three to see *Romeo and Juliet* at the New Theatre, partly as a 'thank you' for the Thanksgiving weekend. It's quite the thing to go to at the moment apparently, and all the cast are very young. Juliet is played by a beautiful actress called Peggy Ashcroft, and Laurence Olivier is Romeo. It was just too romantic, and we were all crying buckets by the end. It helped that I knew the play quite well because we'd read it and then acted it out in class when we were in the third form. I don't think Tara had ever seen anything quite like it: she seemed completely overwhelmed, and hardly said a word in the cab as we took her home afterwards.

"Maybe there'd be a point in having a boyfriend," I whispered to Sarah as the curtain came down after the first act, "if he looked like Laurence Olivier."

"Providing he promised to wear a bow tie," she whispered back. I had to find a hanky quickly, to stifle my giggles.

Saturday 4th January 1936

Second treat yesterday afternoon – and a really Christmassy one too. Mother, Father and I went to see *Scrooge* at the Ritz cinema in Edgware, sitting in the best seats with ice cream and chocolates. The film was quite good, and the scene where Tiny Tim dies is a real weepie. However the same actor was playing Scrooge as a young man and as an old man, and it didn't really work, because you could see that in real life he actually was quite ancient.

Before the main programme started, they showed some Pathé News film of Germany. There were soldiers goose-stepping up and down in perfect formation around a square surrounded by colossal new buildings, and Mr Hitler with that funny moustache of his, taking the salute and then giving a speech in a voice that rose from being soft and soothing to frighteningly loud. He banged his fist on the lectern, and wiped the spittle away from his mouth, and then began all over again. On every side were long flags hanging to the ground decorated with that strange symbol the Germans have – the swastika. In between the pictures of the soldiers were long sequences of the crowds watching the parade. Everyone seemed very beautiful and proud, but rather fanatical. They were all cheering Hitler like mad. It was quite unnerving really, and my mind went back to what Mr Macdonald had said that night at the Embassy.

I don't know what should be done about the Olympics. I can see both sides. Sometimes I think Hitler is so dangerous that it's inevitable we'll be at war with Germany again one day, just like we were twenty years ago, and then the idea of the Games being held in Berlin seems ridiculous. And other times I think the only way we can draw him in and make him see sense is to keep talking to him, in which case we should definitely go and take part. Wouldn't it just be our bad luck if they are cancelled. Though I suppose I'd still only be twenty in 1940 when the next Olympics come round. I've heard the Games may be held in Japan, which would be very exciting. I know quite a few German phrases, but not a word of Japanese.

Monday 13th January 1936

The 'mock' exam results were posted today, and what do you think? I am, according to Mother, officially a clever girl, because they were all so, so much better than back in November, even maths. What a relief! I was actually top in English, and second in history, so all that revising has paid off handsomely. The one small, nagging doubt is that we've not been swimming much over the last couple of months, so of course I may just have convinced Miss Bowes that I really can't do both things well at the same time. I shall just have to prove her wrong, shan't I?

We've started training again. We'd avoided Mrs Williams on the first day back at school, but her unmistakable voice boomed across the hall at us before lunch on Friday, "A word please, ladies?"

Heads turned to see exactly which ladies were being summoned. We knew, of course. Tara raised an eyebrow at me and giggled. She hasn't quite got used to some of the ways of British teachers yet.

"How are we all feeling?" Mrs Williams continued, at a level which ensured the whole school would know about her enquiry. "Still weighed down with too much Christmas stodge, I expect."

We muttered that we were quite well, thank you very much and it was lovely to be back.

"I've had an extremely good idea," she said, "for getting your New Year off to a flying start..."

The good idea turned out to be a training session for forty-five minutes before school three days a week. I gave an involuntary groan.

"Are you a woman or a mouse, Eleanor?" Mrs Williams said, her voice bouncing back off the far wall of the luncheon hall.

"I think perhaps I have distant relations with rodent tendencies," I replied, which is the nearest thing to a joke I've ever tried out on her.

"Won't the Baths mind opening up for us at eight o'clock?" Sarah asked, slightly desperately.

"Not if I ask them, they won't," came the implacable answer.

And so it was that with snow falling gently from the sky and the first cars of the morning skidding crazily down Edgware High Street, Sarah and I met at the station at a quarter to seven today. We didn't do more than grunt at each other until the not-yet-very-well-heated water of the St Pancras Baths woke us up good and proper.

Tuesday 21st January 1936

It's been the strangest day, with everyone and everything so unnaturally quiet. There's been no running in the corridors, no idle chatter, no jokes made, and the school has never seemed so dark and sombre.

Father had warned Mother and me at the weekend that he'd understood from people who should know that the King's life was in danger. Then we heard the doctor say on the radio yesterday evening: *'The King's life is moving peacefully towards its close'*, but it was still a shock to see the headlines on the newspaper stands. King George the Fifth died last night.

"Actually, I'm surprised it hasn't happened before now," Father had said. "He was lucky to get away with a bad case of blood poisoning seven years ago, and apparently his chest has always been weak. Now may God help us all."

Father has never had much time for the Prince of Wales, who'll be our new King Edward the Eighth. He likes Prince Albert, the Duke of York, much better. "A steady chap," he's said of Prince Albert more than once. But I don't know quite what makes the other prince so 'unsteady'. Something to do with women, I expect. It always is, if grown-ups won't talk about it. I know Prince Edward isn't married.

The King's body is going to lie in state in Westminster Hall, where we had our Speech Day last year, and then there'll be a funeral in Windsor next week.

"Shall we go down to Westminster to pay our respects, my dear?" Father asked my mother.

Mother shook her head. She avoids anything to do with death if she can. It always brings back memories of my brother.

"Very well," Father said. "I may have to be there at the funeral, at any rate."

That surprised me, and I was rather sorry about Mother's answer, though I didn't feel I could say anything. I should have quite liked to go and see what a dead king looks like. It doesn't happen every day. And to see a dead body, when it's not someone you really care about, might be a good thing to do.

Monday 17th February 1936

Here I am sitting in bed at home instead of having fun with Sarah and Tara at CCS, and I don't mind saying I'm still feeling very poorly indeed. At least I feel a bit better than I did last week, which wouldn't be very difficult. I've got the dreaded chickenpox which has been going round recently, and it's not the nice friendly illness people make it out to be, I can tell you. Sarah had it when she was four, so she's being allowed to come and see me later, but Tara's banned from all contact. At least she's written me a lovely newsy letter.

The thing is, training was going so well, and school was going so well, and it's really knocked me for six. Mother says I mustn't expect to go back to school or even think about swimming this week and probably next, and at the moment I'm as weak as a kitten. It's as much as I can do to stagger downstairs for toast and tea each afternoon. And I look a complete fright. There are spots all over me, and the ones on my face are turning into moon craters. All in all it's just too awful, and I could cry, I really could.

I suppose I wasn't feeling too bright the weekend before last, but like the new good-girl me, I dragged myself off to school on the Monday and into the Baths as per normal for our early morning session. Mrs Williams has us very organized now. We warm up slowly, and then she does some work on the quality of our front crawl, making sure we get the most out of our breathing and position in the water, keeping our heads right down and pulling the whole way back with our arms. She's making us practise breathing on both sides alternately too, which is a new thing the Japanese swimmers are doing. Once you get used to it, it really helps. Then it's speed work, practising short sprints and building up the distances as we go. Mrs Williams times everything, and keeps telling us how fast we are, and how much faster she wants us to go. It's quite odd. We've got very good at swimming seventy-second lengths to order. How does the brain know how to do that?

Last Monday she wasn't at all happy with me.

"Buck your ideas up, Eleanor," she bawled, clicking her stopwatch irritably. "What's the matter with you today? Put some effort into it. You're way off the pace."

But no matter how much I tried, I felt as if I was going backwards through the water. My legs seemed impossibly heavy, and suddenly I knew I just couldn't swim another stroke. I wanted just to give up, sink into the chlorine depths and die. I thrashed over to the pool side like a novice, only to find I couldn't pull myself out of the water. Credit to Mrs Williams, she quickly saw something was up and was there in a trice to haul me out, but when I tried to stand up on the pool side my legs gave way, and I crashed down onto the tiles. I didn't pass out, but it was a near thing. They swathed me in towels, and bundled me into my clothes, but I was so ill and vague that a cab had to be called to take me home to Edgware. Even Bagshaw the school nurse wasn't completely horrible, so I must have looked grim. Then next day the spots started arriving, so at least Mother knew I hadn't got consumption or beri-beri.

That's it! No energy to write any more. Sorry. That's the way I am at the moment.

Saturday 29th February 1936

Maybe I'm better. I felt I just had to get out the diary and write something since today's the extra day for Leap Year, and somehow I don't think I'll keep a journal going for another four years. Silly me, I was never going to be in school this past week anyway, because it was half-term, but instead (which was rather a surprise!) school came to me in the shape of Mrs Williams. Wasn't that kind of her? She's a funny old stick with that huge foghorn voice and jolly hockey manner she often puts on. But she's very kind, and very ambitious for us too. I wonder what Mr Williams is like? Most of the teachers at CCS are unmarried: the school is their whole life, which means they think it should be our whole life too. Mrs W. seems to leave school behind when she walks out of the gates. She's becoming quite different with the three of us when we're at the Baths, friendlier and less formal, even if her voice is just as loud.

So suddenly on Thursday morning there she was in our front room, quite unannounced as far as I was concerned (though I have an inkling she must have phoned Mother the previous day).

"How are you feeling, Eleanor?" she asked.

"Up and down," I answered. Actually I'd been feeling a lot more 'down' than 'up'. I'm stronger than I was, but I'm finding it quite hard to feel positive about things. The weather hasn't helped: cold, wet and windy. Oh, and I still look like an extra from a horror movie. I'm not the kind of girl who spends every other minute looking in the mirror, but at the moment when I do, it's rather depressing.

"I'm not surprised," Mrs W. said. "I remember having chickenpox myself when I was a youngster, and it's not much fun. I seem to recall being very annoyed with grown-ups telling me it was nothing more than a scratch really, better to get it over and done with, etc. etc."

"The thing is," I said, "I was feeling really on top of things in the swimming pool. And now it's going to be back to square one, with all the work for this season probably wasted.

I'll never pull things back now."

Of course it's more than that too. If there was ever really any prospect of swimming for Britain this year, and maybe in the Olympics – it seems to me that went out of the window with the arrival of the first spot.

"Nonsense," she said comfortingly. "At your age the body recovers remarkably quickly. I'm not sure you and Sarah quite realise how well you're doing. You'll both be there and thereabouts come midsummer. You've got a couple of months before the first of the early-season competitions, and if it's selection for Berlin that's worrying you, my advice in any case would have been to see how it goes. You can't rush these things."

She looked me straight in the eye.

"I'm going to sound like a proper teacher now, but you've got your General Exams in May and June, which must be the number one priority. Welcome to the life of an athlete, young Eleanor. It's as much about recovering from setbacks, injuries, illness and the fact that the dog's died, as it is about winning races. What you never see are the problems other swimmers are having. Believe me, technically, you're just coming to the boil. There's still a good chance!"

I smiled weakly, and tried to exercise a bit of faith.

"You like going to the cinema, don't you?"

I nodded.

"Well, if you want a bit of bucking up, get your parents to take you to see *Anna Karenina*."

This seemed strange. I'd read about the film in Father's *Daily Telegraph*, but it didn't seem like Mrs Williams' cup of tea.

"You won't regret it, I promise you."

And with that, she made her excuses and was off out of the door.

The review of the film had made it sound good, and I needed an outing, so Mother and I went to see it last night. The main feature itself was all right, although a bit slushy for my taste, if I'm honest, with Greta Garbo making big eyes at everyone. What Mrs Williams had wanted me to see, I'm sure, was the news film which came before it. I knew that while I'd been ill the Winter Olympics had taken place in Germany, but to be honest I'd not paid attention to the results. There were lots of dramatic pictures of ski-jumping, although one ski-jump looks much like another to me. What caught my eye was the figure-skater Sonja Henie. She looked so graceful and poised as she won the competition, and it was the third time in a row that she'd collected the gold medal. The first time she competed she'd only been eleven. Can you believe that? And then there was the British ice-hockey team, who surprisingly won gold, just pipping the Canadians, who were so cross, and such bad sports. The Canadians had scored hundreds of goals against everyone, and the British had only just crept through the opening rounds, but somehow in the final they managed to cling on to win. It was truly inspiring to see, and made me feel proud to be British. I came out of the cinema a foot or so taller

77

and thinking to myself, 'Yes, I want to do that. I can do that! I can be a champion.'

Mother gave me a funny look as we walked up towards Seymour Lodge.

"I think maybe you're feeling better," she said.

Tuesday 24th March 1936

"After that, girls, I think we deserve a treat," Tara said as we slouched into school following an especially hard early-morning swim. "Can you get passes from your parents for a trip out to Richmond on Saturday?"

"What's at Richmond?" asked Sarah.

"I'm beginning to think I know London better than you guys," Tara replied. "The ice rink! Most of the American ice-hockey team who should have won the gold medal at the Olympics are playing your lucky limeys on Saturday afternoon. It's a grudge match. Should be good."

Sarah and I had never been to an ice-hockey match, and getting to Richmond isn't too difficult by tube even though it's the opposite side of London, so the various parents were persuaded. Genuinely, I just assumed Mr or Mrs McDonald would be there along with Tara but what she hadn't mentioned was that our chaperones for the trip were to be her two brothers and a tall man in a lounge suit from the American Embassy called Kirk. Kirk said no more than about a dozen words all afternoon, but his eyes flickered this way and that every moment he was with us.

"Secret service," Tara had whispered as we took our seats next to the chilly ice rink. "It would never do if I was kidnapped."

I didn't know if she was joking or not. I've never seen Kirk or anyone like him near CCS. But maybe he's just good at his job!

There's not a lot of comparison between the game we play at school ('field hockey' as Tara calls it) and what we saw on Saturday. Ice hockey is played at a million miles an hour – so fast that at first it was hard to see the puck as it whizzed across the ice – and extremely roughly. The rougher it got the more Tara seemed to like it. She whistled and shouted when the players banged into each other, which was usually on purpose, I thought, and generally made an exhibition of herself. Sarah and I sat there quietly, like good English girls.

"Aren't you enjoying it?" Tara asked at the end of the first period of play. The Americans were leading 2–1.

"It's great," I said brightly. "Lovely."

"Doesn't seem like you are," she answered, a bit crestfallen that we weren't whooping and hollering along.

It didn't help me to enter into the spirit of things that

Harrison, Tara's brother, was sitting very close to me in the next seat. He seemed to spend as much time watching me as the game, and to be honest, by the time the final whistle went, I was a bit fed up with his attention. Also, the US team won easily and Tara was slightly too happy about that.

Afterwards, as we ate ice cream ... (Of course! What else would you scoff after two hours shivering by the ice rink?) ... conversation turned to how the American and Canadian ice-hockey teams had been really so much better than us Brits at the Olympics. Then suddenly we were talking about the possibility of Sarah and me going to Berlin, which I really didn't want to discuss because I'm getting superstitious, and talking about it seems to make it so much less likely to happen. Harrison and Tara were harping on about 'should we go, shouldn't we go?' and frankly that old chestnut's beginning to turn into sour grapes, because Tara definitely can't and we just perhaps might. Then it suddenly came to me.

"Hang on," I said. "In the end your American ice-hockey team turned up at Garmisch looking like butter wouldn't melt in their mouths, and according to you they should have won the gold medal. So what's different about our British swimmers going to Berlin?"

Oh, said Tara, that was only the Winter Olympics, and didn't count, which seemed a pathetic argument to me.

"Anyway," said Harrison loftily, "it's different now. Two

weeks ago the Germans invaded the Rhineland. They've broken the terms of the Treaty of Versailles."

"So?" I said, a bit flustered. "What does that change?"

"It shows they can't be trusted."

Harrison pronounced on this as if he were the American ambassador. I couldn't shake him off, all the way back to the tube. He was beside me every inch of the walk. He even tried to hold my hand as we came down the steps out of the ice rink, pretending to be worried I might slip. Ugh!

"I think he really does like you," giggled Sarah as the District Line train bumped the two of us towards Charing Cross.

"So Tara says," I grunted. "Well, I don't like Harrison."

I quickly changed the subject.

"How are your aunt and uncle in Berlin?"

Sarah's face clouded.

"Not so good. The other week Auntie Hanna wrote to say that the front door of their flat had been defaced. Someone had painted 'Death to Jews' on it. She's very frightened. The mood on the streets is very threatening. And when Uncle Jakob plays piano in the bar, people are always making fun of him. On one occasion recently some drunken idiot took his glasses off his face while he was playing and stamped on them. For no reason at all! And the people standing around just laughed."

"Can't Hanna and Jakob come to England?"

"I think you need a permit to leave. And it costs money which they don't have."

"Couldn't your family help?"

Her face fell further, and immediately I felt awful, because it was clearly the wrong question.

"Oh, Ellie, I wish they could. But Daddy's business is falling apart, and I'm not even sure we'll be able to stay in the house at Stonegrove. Or that they can afford to keep me at CCS for another two years. Daddy's losing heart, and he and Mummy just shout at each other all the time. I might have to work for him or take a job with someone else. You'd be surprised how many people in England say 'Bloody Jews' and prefer to take their custom elsewhere these days. Sometimes I think what's happening in Germany today will happen in England tomorrow."

"Why didn't you tell me about all this?"

"Oh, you know ... when I'm not at home, all I want to do is think about happy things."

"Look," I said, "you're my best friend, and I will never, never let anything bad happen to you."

She turned in her seat to face me.

"You say that now," she said. "But you don't understand. When things are the way they are in Germany right now, sometimes it's impossible to stand up even for people you love."

Last night I talked to my father about what Sarah had said. He looked serious.

"I'm sorry to hear that," he said. "I gather Mr Rosenthal is rather a good man. I know there's a bit of feeling about the number of Jewish families who've moved here, and I suppose you'd expect that. A lot of folk are still feeling the pinch, and looking for someone to blame."

"Why are Jewish people hated so much?" I asked. "I don't understand it. Sarah's every bit as English as me! She thinks the same, and acts the same. She was more sad than I was when King George died. I expect her father pays his taxes, the way you do."

Father stared at the wall, searching for inspiration.

"Human beings are very sensitive to difference, aren't they?" he said finally. "Think about the prejudice there is even against someone who comes from Yorkshire. Or the difficulty people have accepting that Britain won't rule India for ever. Or the amazement when a West Indian like the footballer Walter Tull or the cricketer Learie Constantine not only shows himself to be a great sportsman, but an honourable and clever person too. Or consider the time it took for women to be allowed to vote. I was brought up to think that most of these things were impossible. But I'm finding this dog must learn new tricks ... it's a different world."

His voice trailed off for a moment.

"What I'm trying to say is ... even at my age I'm still learning that I don't know it all, and that sometimes I'm wrong. But it's hard. Sometimes I feel my tribe is being threatened by all this change. Anyway, enough of this. We must hope some way can be found to help the Rosenthals."

Easter Monday, 13th April 1936

It's Easter Bank Holiday Monday and here I am sitting at the desk in my bedroom revising, just as I've been doing every other day of the Easter holiday. My life right now is nothing but working and swimming. To my surprise I'm finding I quite enjoy concentrating so hard, but for a few minutes I'm going to give myself a break from being the perfect student to tell you what a hero my father is.

On Good Friday each year there's always a long afternoon service at St. Margaret's, and although I hate it because it's always such a dark and sad time, with the church stripped bare of flowers and decoration and everyone in solemn clothes, there's never any getting out of going along with Mother and Father. The Rector hasn't been well, so instead we had a very peculiar man by the name of the Rev. Dalrymple in charge, whom no one had ever seen before. Instead of one long sermon, there was a series of shorter sermonettes with some gloomy hymns spread between them. Normally

I'd be so bored that I'd almost fall asleep, but Friday turned out to be completely riveting. The Dalrymple man, who was tall, stooped and greyly gaunt, was talking about how Jesus was betrayed and crucified just as it says in the Bible, but as he talked he kept becoming all emotional. I thought he was going to burst into tears at any moment. The thing is, he kept coming back to how it was all the Jews' fault that Jesus had been killed, and how they'd never repented and they'd still do it today if they had the chance. I must say, thinking about my gentle friend Sarah, I thought this was pretty awful since she certainly wouldn't hurt a fly.

I was sitting next to Father, and even the first time the Rev. Dalrymple went off on this tack, I could feel him going all stiff and tense as if he was really uncomfortable with what was being said. Second time round Father was shifting about on the pew and clearing his throat. I could see his face reddening with anger. He was swallowing hard, and looking one minute at his feet and the next at the ceiling. Mother glanced across at him anxiously. She put a hand gently on his arm. When Dalrymple started off on his theme a third time, saying that the Jews had brought upon themselves what was happening in Germany, suddenly Father was standing up, his whole body absolutely shaking with anger. I went hot and cold both at once, wondering what on earth was going to happen now. It seemed to take a moment for anyone including the Rev. Dalrymple to notice anything amiss, but when Father's voice thundered out across the church, everyone's head jerked around in unison as if a gun had been let off. You just don't do this sort of thing in church, particularly at safe, respectable St Margaret's and especially not if you're the churchwarden, however much you may disagree with a sermon.

"This is an outrage," my father began. "How dare you come to a place of which you know nothing to speak such blatant and dangerous nonsense. You should be ashamed."

There were embarrassed mutterings amongst the congregation, and someone behind us said quite audibly, "Sit down, man. You're making a fool of yourself."

My father half-turned and continued, "Even if you will, sir, I will not sit idly by and listen to Evil finding its voice in Edgware. What happened two thousand years ago is truly done and in the past. No one now can be blamed or held accountable. But Christ is crucified anew where we allow evil to go unchallenged – by us!"

"You're a disgrace," said the other man. "You're not fit to be churchwarden. Be quiet and listen to the voice of scripture and authority."

"You may believe this man speaks with authority but I at any rate shall not stay to give support to such ill-conceived words," stormed my father, gesturing at the pulpit. "You remain silent if you will." And with that, he bent to pick up his coat, and stepped out of the pew. He waited as my mother gathered her handbag and gloves, and with heads held high the three of us left the church, our feet echoing loudly on the stone floor.

We none of us said a word as we walked home, but as my father opened the front door of Seymour Lodge, he turned and said quietly but firmly, "I will resign, too..." And then with a rather dark chuckle he added, "Although I don't suppose I have much choice now."

It has always meant a lot to Father to be churchwarden, but what he did on Friday was so noble and right I can't tell you how much I admire him.

I know something now that I didn't a year ago. Back then adults always seemed so certain and unchanging. If you knew what they thought at any moment, it seemed you could depend on it for always. But I've seen Father's opinions change about this matter in just a few months, as surely as spring has burst out into daffodils and blossom from the darkness and death of winter. Can I dare to think I and Sarah have had anything to do with it?

Wednesday 22nd April 1936

I have a plan for the new term, and it's written on a wall calendar I've made which hangs in my bedroom, so that I see it every morning when I wake up. On it are the dates of exams, littered threateningly through the month of June, and the swimming events in which we're going to compete during May and early July. And there's a red dotted ring round August 4th, which on Monday Mrs Williams let slip is the day the British swimming team will set out for Berlin. It's a dotted ring because I refuse to allow myself to think it's possible we'll be with them.

I feel so fit now – particularly compared to the way I was in February – bright-eyed and bushy-tailed, as Mother always likes to say. On the few days I don't swim, I make sure I run, which is something I never did before. I'm surprised to find it makes me feel really good. I actually have more energy for school work afterwards. I don't understand that: you'd think I'd be worn out, wouldn't you!

Slowly, slowly, our times are improving in the baths, two fifths of a second quicker here, half a second there.

"You're British swimming's best kept secrets," Mrs

Williams keeps saying to us with a smile. "Won't you just surprise a few people later in the summer! I can't wait."

She clearly relishes the thought. Her Great Plan is to get us up to speed during May to just about qualify for the Amateur Swimming Association championships at Wembley in early July, and then to amaze the world with our times there, when we've had a nice rest from swimming by tackling our exams. Tara is being a great sport. She won't be able to swim at Wembley even if she's fast enough – because of being American – but she's pushing us all the way. And she's said no more about the question of whether swimmers should go to Berlin. I'm not sure I'd be such a loyal friend if I was her.

"I want you to concentrate on the 440 freestyle," Mrs Williams says. "It's our weakest event. And it'll have shock value when they see you swimming that distance fast, because there are still a lot of people who think girls aren't strong enough. But both you and Sarah have excellent endurance."

Because of this probably sadly mistaken view, she regularly puts us through the pain of swimming a mile straight off, yelling our split times to us every length of the bath.

"Wouldn't we be better sticking to a hundred-yard thrash?" I occasionally try out with her, as we pull ourselves out of the water to sprawl on the pool side tiles like beached whales, arms, thighs and calves aching.

"Trust me," she says with a glint in her eye. "Teacher knows best." Mrs Williams is an extraordinarily determined woman, but what I like about her is, she never, ever gets cross with us, however well or badly we perform.

So, diary, you're not going to hear very much from me for the next couple of months. I'm organized. I'm committed. My brain is going to be somewhere else. Farewell and adieu!

Tuesday 26th May 1936

Even when we first moved out to Seymour Lodge, we didn't have a telephone in the house. I was thinking only the other day how amazing it is to be able to talk to someone miles away on the other side of London. How did people manage when they had to write to someone before they paid them a visit? – which Grandpa still always does, on the rare occasions he gets together with his old cronies.

When I said cheerio to Sarah last Friday (it's the beginning of the half-term holiday, and we've sworn not to bother each other until Thursday so that we can revise) she said, "Did you know your father telephoned my father last weekend?"

"No. Why?"

"I haven't a clue. But I overheard him saying thanks and

goodbye. The strange thing is, he didn't say anything to me about it. He sounded very cheerful – as if it had been a very jolly conversation!"

And my father hadn't said anything to me either. So, the first thing I'll write about telephones, if by any chance the subject comes up in my English language exam next week, is that they encourage secrecy. I'm itching to know what the two fathers said to each other, but I know I can't ask if neither of them will say.

There was a telephone call for me too on Saturday, from Harrison MacDonald, and I can tell you, that pretty much floored me. My mother took the call, and having shouted up the stairs for me to come down, she handed me the receiver with a broad and unmotherly smirk.

"It's for you," she said. "How exciting!"

I don't think Harrison is very used to talking to girls apart from Tara, for all that he makes out he's so much the man-about-town. He stammered and coughed all the way through our chat, even though I was trying to be my nicest self – not for any other reason, you understand, than that he was so obviously embarrassed. Apparently he was ringing to say 'good luck' with the exams, adding between a lot of throat-clearing that perhaps we could go to the pictures together when the exams were done with.

Actually I think I'd die of boredom, because I can't imagine what we'd talk about. I said to him that of course it would be lovely but I wasn't sure that my parents would let me (I was pretty sure Mother was listening behind the door from the hall into the lounge), and that anyway, as I'm sure Tara would have told him, I had a lot of swimming commitments in July. He was being perfectly sweet, but honestly! I wondered if Tara had put him up to it. It's just the kind of thing she'd think would be funny.

"Harrison sounds like a nice young man," my mother said later.

I pulled a face.

"Plenty of fish in the sea," she said airily.

"But not in the swimming pool," I added, which made her laugh.

"You might regret it in a few years' time," she said. "When he's very rich!"

I pulled another face.

So the second thing you could say in an essay about telephones is that they open the doors to all kinds of conversations you might not want to have. You see the way my mind is working. At the moment everything revolves around these wretched exams.

Sarah and I have swum competitively three times in May, at Hampstead, Croydon and Watford. At Croydon we were up against two well-known swimmers, Gladys Morcom and Zilpha Grant, who the papers say will both make the Olympic team. They had the beating of us over a quarter-mile although by barely a couple of seconds in a slow race. I came third and Sarah was fifth. Gladys and Zilpha were very complimentary, and lots of people we didn't know said "Well done!" in a rather patronizing way, as if it was just a piece of good luck really and wouldn't ever happen again.

Perhaps because we know Hampstead, we swam very well there and came an easy first and second. I very nearly broke through six minutes five seconds for the first time in competition (although I think I've swum faster in practice). But at Watford I was very out of sorts, and a third-placed Sarah touched in just in front of me. The field wasn't very strong, and Mrs Williams was probably a bit cross with us for swimming so badly but didn't want to let it show. We've ditched our old horrible old woollen suits when we race now. Instead we swim in the newer silk ones which feel a lot nicer in the water, and at least make you think you're going faster. However, after the Watford race we suddenly noticed something of a kerfuffle developing between Mrs Williams and the judges. Hands and arms were waving about rather a lot, and voices were definitely raised. We looked at each other and decided to keep our heads down – we were a bit fed up with the way we'd swum. Apparently Mrs Williams had put in a complaint about the costume of the girl who'd come second in front of Sarah.

"Girl wasn't wearing anything underneath," she said brusquely afterwards. "I told them. Rules are rules. Firstly it's rather disgusting. Secondly it probably made her swim faster because she was more streamlined."

Sarah raised an eyebrow at me. Mrs Williams is so competitive. The judges gave in and disqualified the poor girl so we came second and third, but was it worth it for one place, when we really didn't deserve it?

Next week the exams begin. I have dreadful butterflies already. I feel just the way I do standing on the edge of the pool waiting to dive in at the beginning of a race. But far, far worse!

Tuesday 30th June 1936

They're done. They're finished. No more maths or physics. I shan't ever have to worry about triangles of forces or simultaneous equations ever again. I can't tell you how light-headed and happy I felt when we walked out of the hall at the end of the second maths paper yesterday afternoon. Sarah and I literally danced our way out of school and down the road, more like five-year-olds than fifteen-year-olds.

Mostly I think I've done all right. The annoying exam was history, at which I'm usually really good. Everyone thought it a very difficult paper. I worry that I misunderstood one of the questions, and I know (Big Sin!) I ran out of time when I was writing the last one, but fingers crossed I've done enough.

So now all that's left on my wallchart are the Amateur Swimming Association championships at the Empire Pool in Wembley, which start tomorrow, and then that fading dotted ring round August 4th. Sarah, Tara and I swam with Mrs Williams for the first time in a week this afternoon. Afterwards, when we'd changed back into our school togs, rather to our amazement she said, "Well done girls. Let's go and celebrate with a cup of tea," so we walked together down to Upton's teashop, which is quite smart by Camden's standards. It was all a bit strange sitting there in public with Mrs Williams. Perhaps this is what being in the Sixth Form is like all the time!

"Well, the exams don't seem to have done you much harm," she said. "Your times are holding up quite well."

We muttered tactfully about being glad, surprised, etc.

"So the question is then, Eleanor and Sarah, how will things go on Saturday?"

More muttering.

"Have you been to the Empire Pool before?"

Neither of us had. The pool opened two years ago, and it's supposed to be absolutely vast, and of course all kinds of day swimmers go there just to take in the sights. I'm not being snobby but people like us wouldn't normally go there unless there was a good reason.

"It's a very big place," said Mrs Williams. "So don't be put off by that. And of course there'll be a few more spectators than you're used to. It's not the fastest pool in the world either. You might find the water a bit heavy: they chlorinate it to death so that nobody's little Jemima or Johnny catches anything they shouldn't."

"How many heats will there be?" I asked.

"Two," Mrs W. answered. "All the good swimmers will be there – Olive Bartle, Margaret Jeffrey, Gladys Morcom, Joan Turner. Morcom's in excellent form, and so is Bartle. You'll have to swim very well to beat them. But steady, the Buffs: if you can swim the times of which you're capable, you both have a good chance of making the top three. Just put your thinking caps on, and don't go out too early."

Easy to say. Not so easy to do!

Sunday 5th July 1936

Gloom and desolation. So much for the fine thoughts of foreign travel and overnight success. After all the work, all the planning, neither of us even made the final at Wembley yesterday. Whether it was all the worry I don't know, but as soon as I woke up yesterday morning I knew it wouldn't be my day. I had a vague headache, and my legs felt all wrong, and although I remembered what Mrs Williams said, and kept my energy for the second half of my heat, I'd left myself far too much to do, and came in fourth, just outside the six minutes ten seconds required for the final. Sarah, on the other hand, forgot everything Mrs W. said. She was leading the other heat with a hundred yards to go, and then utterly and completely blew up to finish fifth. I honestly think she could have broken six minutes if she'd been a bit more patient. Gladys Morcom sailed away in the final to win by miles in five minutes fifty seconds, which puts our swims into proportion, doesn't it?

"Oh, bother," Sarah moaned afterwards. "Why do I have porridge for a brain?"

Mrs Williams overheard the comment. "I don't know why you have porridge for a brain, young Sarah, except that you do. No use crying over spilt milk. It was just a mistake, but it's not the end of the world. And when all's said and done, the other competitors were far more experienced than you. You'll be back for glory in four years' time."

"There may never be a 'four years' time,'" Sarah muttered ruefully.

I have to say, I do feel pretty miserable. Mrs Williams was very nice about it all, but as she's always said, you have to take your chances when they come, and the plain fact is that we didn't. And what if Miss Bowes was right all along and the exams have gone badly because we've been splitting our time between swimming and study? The more I think about it, the more I can convince myself I've made a total mess of things this summer. As Sarah says, "Oh bother!" I'm lying here in my bedroom staring at the ceiling. I don't feel like doing anything, not even reading a book, not even a Rose Gershwin. And the worst thing is, the exam results don't come out until the end of August, so the whole of the holidays will have been completely spoiled, *regretting!*

Wednesday 15th July 1936

I've been like a bear with a sore head these past ten days, I really have, but now I've got the most extraordinary and wonderful thing to tell you. I know just how Cinderella felt. Sarah and I are going to the Olympics after all. A telegram arrived at each of our houses this morning. It simply read 'Congratulations Stop Leave for Berlin 4th Aug Stop Details follow from Mrs W Stop'

I stared and stared, and still didn't understand. The last places in the Olympic swimming team had been filled – I'd seen the names in *The Times* on Monday evening – so how could I be going too? I handed the telegram to Mother, who immediately put a dampener on things. She frowned as she read.

"I wouldn't get your hopes too high," she said dubiously. "You'll have to talk to your father about this."

I was about to go into an adolescent sulk, and start shouting about how could she say such a thing after all the hard work etc. etc., but fortunately the telephone rang at that point. It was Mrs Williams, and when Mother started talking to her, Mrs W. was obviously being so nice that it was impossible for Mother to be difficult. When I finally got a word in edgeways with my own teacher, Mrs W. explained.

"You're quite right. All the places for the medal competitions are filled," she said. "And I don't think we were expecting anything else, were we, after the Wembley race? But they're going to hold a demonstration race over fifteen hundred metres for women, and they particularly want to show off younger swimmers. So you and Sarah are the obvious choices to go with the British team. Well done, Ellie. It's a marvellous opportunity for you. I'm so proud."

I spent the day agonizing about how Father would take the news. I needn't have worried.

"That's wonderful," he said. "We'll have to come to watch."

"Is that possible?" I asked in astonishment.

"I'm owed some leave," he replied. "And for once in my life I should think I can pull some strings. The Office may even think it a helpful thing for me to go at a time like this."

Whoever the Office are, I thought to myself, well, bully for them.

"And is Sarah Rosenthal going too?" he asked.

I said she was, and Mrs Williams would be there, as part of the team management.

"Well that's good," he added quickly. "So you'll have some company." But there was a strange look in his eye. I thought then that he was keeping something back from me.

Monday 3rd August 1936

My bag is packed, and I'm ready for the off, but so completely nervous that I can't sit still. I shouldn't think I'll sleep a wink tonight. What will Germany be like? And will the other swimmers be nice to us? We've said hello to a few of them at competitions, like Margaret Jeffrey and Gladys Morcom, but we've never spent any time with them. Now we'll be together practically every minute of the day for a whole fortnight. And we'll be the babies of the team too. They'll probably just ignore us, or perhaps think we're silly.

"It'll be wonderful fun. You'll enjoy it when you get there," Mother said, but I could see even she wasn't too sure.

(We're friends again after she was such a misery about the telegram.) "I honestly didn't know what your father would think," she admitted. "And I couldn't presume, could I? He has to have the final say about these things, after all."

I'd wanted to ask why, but couldn't of course. It's Mother who's always championed my swimming. In all the years Father has only been to see me race just once or twice. If girls are being educated to be the equals of boys, why should it be men who make all the decisions? Sometime when the Olympics are over, I shall have to pluck up courage to ask him to explain that one.

Sarah and I won't get to swim our race until Friday week, so the plan seems to be for Mother and Father to fly out the Wednesday after next and come home on the Saturday, two days before we return with the rest of the team. I hope I can make their trip worthwhile.

And one other thing. Tara telephoned to wish us luck. Wasn't that nice of her? I don't think I'd be so generous if I was in her shoes – I'd just feel miserable and jealous.

"Knock 'em dead," she said, "Even if they come from Boston. Just for your race only, I'm supporting the Brits. See ya!"

Wednesday 5th August 1936

If Sarah weren't here as well, I don't know what I'd do. I'm so miserable and cold and shocked. I suppose I'd imagined that when we got to Berlin we'd be staying in a grand hotel like the one in Bournemouth. I didn't expect that we girls would all be sleeping together in a long dormitory, stuffing our fingers in our ears to shut out the snoring, and sharing cold showers with a crowd of Dutch and Belgians who speak very little English. When I was small I made Mother and Father promise faithfully that they'd never send me away to boarding school because I was so terrified of just this kind of thing, and now here I am even further away from home than I'd be in Brighton or Cheltenham. I could cry. The beds are wooden and the mattresses are made of straw, like something out of Hans Christian Andersen, and the food for dinner this evening was so awful I simply couldn't eat any at all. There was some kind of boiled meat with tinned vegetables, and a congealed rice pudding for afters. I wasn't the only one who pushed her plate away, and there was a bit of mumbling amongst the girls when we got down from dinner. It's ten o'clock at night and officially 'lights out' now, but I'm writing this under a thin cover by the light of a torch. I've got a jumper on over my pyjamas because I'm so chilled. I can see Sarah hunched up in the bed next to me. I don't think she's asleep yet either, and I know she's just as miserable as I am, because when we got into our beds she reached out and clung on fiercely to my hand. How are we going to survive the next ten days? I bet the German swimmers aren't living half-starved in a prison-camp dormitory.

We met Mrs Williams and a few of the swimming team at Liverpool Street Station in London yesterday evening. To begin with it was all a great adventure. The train didn't arrive at Harwich docks until past our usual bedtimes, and we were a bit bleary-eyed as we climbed up the gangplank of the *Prague* to find our berths. Mrs Williams had wangled us a cabin for two with real portholes – not that we could see anything out of them!

"This is amazing," Sarah said throwing her bag onto the bed. "I feel really important. And now we're here, I don't want to go to sleep. Let's go and explore."

So we wandered around the decks and through the restaurant as the ship began to plough its way out into the North Sea. I'd been worried I'd be seasick – I've never been on a proper liner before – but the sea was calm and I found I didn't mind the gentle rolling. Eventually we ran into Mrs Williams, who'd probably been down to our cabin to check on us only to find we weren't there.

"If I were you, ladies," she said sternly, tapping her watch, "I'd go and get some shut-eye. Who knows what tomorrow will bring!"

What it brought was an early morning docking at the Hook of Holland and a comfortable journey on a smart train right the way through Holland, crossing the German border at about 11.30. Then it was on and on through miles of flat country, past countless villages decked out in German swastika flags, finally arriving at Berlin's Friedrichstrasse Station about half past four. Our party of 30 people had several compartments to itself, and everyone was very jolly and made us feel welcome. There was a lot of singing, some of it with rather rude words (from the men!), which the ladies either chose to ignore or giggle at.

"Close your ears, you two," Margaret Jeffrey said. "If Fanny Williams thinks we've corrupted you, we'll never hear the end of it."

There was a welcoming party at the station, with a lot of smiling girls carrying flowers. There were lots of men in blazers too, including the very recognizable Mr Harold Fern, who used to be the top person in British swimming and now seems to rule the whole swimming world.

"Whatever else you do, and whoever else you meet, up to and including Herr Hitler, for heaven's sake just make sure you're nice to Mr Fern," Mrs Williams had said, "if you know what's good for you." So now when he made a point of coming over to say hello, Sarah curtseyed, which caught me out completely. I did a very peculiar half bend at the waist as if I was nodding to the altar in church, and went all tongue-tied.

A green-painted coach drew up. Some soldiers clambered out and stood to attention by its door.

"Oh, I do like a man in uniform," said Gladys Morcom. "I think I'm going to enjoy Germany."

We shuffled over towards the coach.

"Excuse me ladies," said a German gentleman in very good English, "but this is not for you. Only for the male swimmers who are travelling to the Olympic Village. But you please will go with our young friends." He gestured at the girls with the flowers. "They will take you to your accommodation. It is a tram ride, and then not far to walk."

"Are we not going to the Olympic Village too?" asked Margaret Jeffrey.

"No," the German smiled. "We have a place much better for you. Very close to the swimming stadium. Very convenient and useful."

The tram rattled along for about twenty-five minutes while we took in the sights. There were leafy avenues with people enjoying the evening sunshine. Everywhere behind them on the grand monumental buildings there were flags. They were hanging on poles from windows and by front doors, in rows outside public offices and parks, the red, the black and the swastika never out of sight for a second. There were uniforms everywhere too. It reminded me of Grandpa's collection of wartime photographs from the time when every respectable young man was in the armed forces.

The tram came to the end of its line a few miles outside the city. People were milling around outside in a large open space, waiting for trams and buses.

"We have arrived at the Reichssportfeld," said our escort. "Look over there and you will see the Olympic Stadium for the athletics, and on its far side the swimming stadium. So you see how lucky you are to be so close. And now the White Guides will lead you to your accommodation."

In the middle distance we could see the huge pink marble bowl of the athletics stadium glinting in the low sun, and as we stood and watched we could hear the roar of the crowd drifting towards us in waves of sound.

"I wish we'd been here in time for the opening ceremony," Sarah said. (The Games opened on Saturday and the athletics competitions are already half-completed.)

"Yes, isn't it a shame?" I replied. "I'd have liked the chance to walk out behind our flag in front of all those people. You'd have thought they could have got us here a few days earlier."

We hauled ourselves and our bags along gravel paths behind the bouncing girls with their flowers – the White Guides. We weren't bouncing quite as much, but then we'd been travelling for twenty-four hours with only four hours' sleep.

After ten minutes one of our team, Doris Storey, asked plaintively, "Is it much further?"

"Just a few minutes more..." a guide replied.

After another ten minutes someone else moaned, "My feet are killing me."

"We are there. Very nearly," came the answer. And then we rounded a few bushes and saw the low white-painted buildings of the women's accommodation.

"Well," said Mrs Williams, looking around once we were inside. "It's a bit Spartan, ladies, but I suppose it'll do."

"I suppose it'll have to," said Gladys grimly. "If there's nothing better..."

Thursday 6th August 1936

Things always seem better in the morning, don't they? And actually, I think the whole team had been as shocked as Sarah and I were by the state of affairs when we arrived. But as this morning wore on, after a really nasty porridge breakfast, we began to laugh at it all. None of us could get over the constant attention of the White Guides, or as we've started to call them, the White Guards. Sarah and I seem to have been given one of our very own, called Elke. I think Elke's trying hard to be kind, but there's just something about the way she speaks which makes it seem as if we're only here to be told what to do.

"You will be ready to leave at 9.30," she said yesterday evening. "And you will practise at the swimming stadium from half past ten until half past eleven. You will return to the accommodation at twelve o'clock for lunch at 12.30. Then you can relax until half past two, when we will go sightseeing." (The sightseeing turned out to be another endless walk on gravel paths around the Reichssportfeld.)

Of course this is all really very sensible. To give the swimmers of all the different countries a chance to get used to the swimming pool, the organizers have to give each group a particular time. Nevertheless, the way we were all marched up the path at 9.30 on the dot made us feel as if we'd joined the army.

"One, two, one, two. Pick up your heels you miserable lot. No slacking now!" shouted Gladys from the back. I like Gladys. She's got a very good sense of humour.

Mrs Williams has been lovely. She just quietly checks that we're OK every now and then, but hasn't made a big fuss. I suspect she's told the other girls to keep an eye out for us though.

When Bobby Leivers, one of the men's swimming team, tried to walk back with us at lunchtime, the White Guides stood in his way.

"I'm very sorry. It is not permitted," he was told by a guide half his size. "It is for the women only to go this way." And no amount of sweet-talking would persuade her to change her mind.

"Don't worry about it, Bobby," Gladys shouted at his back. "Plenty of time to let our hair down later. They'll get bored."

It seems as if the men are doing better than we are as far as eating and sleeping are concerned.

"From what I hear," said Margaret Jeffrey indignantly, "they're living in the lap of luxury with all mod. cons.. Good food, waiter service, four to a room, presents from the German people. It's all right for some. Only thing is, they're miles away out in the country. Johnny says the grounds of the Olympic Village are really beautiful, not that we're ever likely to see them."

The swimming stadium is wonderful, and there were huge crowds of people there today, just to watch us train. It's open-air of course, and they say when it's full twenty two thousand people can watch from the raked seating which towers above the swimmers on three sides. The weather improved as we swam, and it was good to get the sun on our backs. The water feels light and the lanes are clearly marked: everything seems right for fast times. The diving pool and the swimming pool are separate, and there's even a smart restaurant behind the diving tower with a view right across the pool. They're having a party for us there tonight.

Of course all the swimmers want to be in the pool as long as they can, and despite the precise instructions there were some heated arguments. From hearing Tara talk about how competitive Americans are it didn't surprise me to hear Yankee voices being raised.

"I'll swim for as long as I d***** well like," said one to a blazered official. "You think you can make me get out?"

"We would be grateful if you could perhaps co-operate, in the spirit of the Olympic movement," came the tactful reply.

"Oh, just tell 'em to sling their hooks," one of our men added.

For the party tonight we'll have to wear our team uniform, including the white pleated skirts and ankle socks! I think we'll look silly, and in my case even younger than I really am.

Friday 7th August 1936

"They don't do much for a girl, but you'll get used to it," Gladys said, yanking the waistband of her skirt a little higher as we climbed the stairs to the Stadium restaurant. "Anyway, you two look just fine. Let's go and talk for England."

The room was crowded, and as we stood by its edge to get

a better view of who was there, Sarah clutched my arm, and gave a small but quite discernible shudder.

"It's Joseph Goebbels," she said, "I'm sure of it. Look, over there."

She pointed to a small dapper man, clean-shaven and with swept-back dark hair, standing on the far side, surrounded by dignitaries. The name rang a bell.

"He's President of the Games, but that's not the half of it," Sarah hissed in my ear. "He's one of the Jew-haters. Perhaps the worst. Hitler's right-hand man. I'm shocked, Ellie. I never expected him to be here. He's one of the ones most responsible for the trouble Auntie Hanna and Uncle Jakob are having!"

Sarah knew one face. Strangely, I recognized another. Standing close to Goebbels was a tall, radiantly beautiful woman. It was Lady Diana Mitford, who you'll remember came to dinner at our house with the odious Mosley the night I got myself into trouble with Father.

We swimmers were rounded up and pushed into line ready to be presented to the great and good, which in this case included Herr Goebbels. Sarah and I were last in the queue.

"Am I going to have to shake that man's hand?" she asked tremulously.

"I don't think we've got much choice, have we? Just do it and get it over with," I said, and immediately regretted my cowardice.

"He talked to you because you're tall and fair, and that's OK with the Nazis," she said in agitation. "What hope is there, Ellie, if they can't even face a conversation with us Jews? You'll see tomorrow. If Fräulein Riefenstahl does turn up, she'll only be interested in pictures of you..."

Sitting there, on our beds in the bare dormitory, I felt awful, separated from my friend, unable to bridge the gap between us that was a simple accident of birth.

True to her word, as we practised this afternoon, Fräulein Riefenstahl did arrive with a tall broad-shouldered cameraman who looked more like a film star himself. They shot some film in a rather careless way as we ploughed up and down, but whether it was of me or Sarah or both of us, I really don't know. At first sight I'd thought she seemed really nice on Thursday evening. But to be honest, this afternoon she was very haughty and distant. She was apparently far more interested in pawing the cameraman. They seemed very taken with each other.

"Well, aren't you the lucky ones," said Gladys as we dried off. "Spoken to personally by the big man last night, and on film this afternoon. You'll end up pinned on someone's wall, if you're not careful."

Sunday 9th August 1936

We trained in the morning and then sunbathed all yesterday afternoon as the swimming events started. There were mixed fortunes for our team. Doris Storey did marvellously well to qualify for the final of the two hundred metres breast stroke, but most of our other swimmers failed even to make the semi-finals.

"Only to be expected," said Mrs Williams, as cheerful as ever. "We're way behind some of the other countries. But if you young 'uns work hard, you'll be up there next time round. Go and watch Mastenbroek if you want to see how it's done."

Rita Mastenbroek is the Dutch swimmer who will win the freestyle events, no doubt about it. In the dormitory she keeps herself to herself. She doesn't waste a word or a moment: you can see she's here in Berlin for one reason only – to be a champion. And out in the pool, every movement is clean and powerful, every stroke identical to the previous one. We watched her cruise home in the heats of the hundred metres. As soon as she'd touched in, she pulled herself out of the pool with no sign of having exerted herself, gathered her things together and was gone in an instant.

"How will we ever compete with that?" Sarah gasped, as the crowd settled back down.

"Let's hope she's retired by 1940," I answered. "Otherwise, I don't think there's any chance..."

Elke came to find us with a message.

"You have a visitor," she said. "I will take you to her."

To our amazement it was Tara, looking exceptionally pleased with herself.

"Whatever are you doing here?" we asked, throwing our arms around each her. Elke stood to one side, frowning.

"I said I'd see you, didn't I?" Tara replied.

"I thought you meant when we got home, not here..." I answered

"Ah well, what's the good of having parents in high places who drag you halfway round the world if you don't get to see the sights," she sighed carelessly. "And I tell you what, I've even managed to get us seats in the athletics stadium tomorrow if you can get time off..."

Elke looked put out (she obviously likes to be the one who organizes everything!) but Mrs Williams was fine about it. From her lack of surprise, I guess she already knew Tara might drop in.

The size of the athletics stadium is deceptive. When you're standing outside you can see only half of it, because inside you suddenly find that the stadium has been built way down into the ground, and as you enter you suddenly realise with a shock that the arena is much, much larger than you ever dreamed.

Tara had got us seats at ninety degrees from the Führer's box. It was the last day of the athletics competition and Herr Hitler himself was expected to attend. The stadium was pretty well full when we arrived and the noise was already deafening, but suddenly the ninety thousand voices in the crowd let rip to such an extent that we had to put our fingers in our ears as the little man dressed in military uniform with a peaked cap took his place alongside his chosen guests. We were close enough to see the familiar moustache, the medals across his chest, the swastika badge on his forearm. Hitler seemed as excited and expectant as anyone, turning around to greet people, banging his fist enthusiastically on the rail in front of him and clapping his hands.

The first event was the men's hundred metres relay final – a race without a British team, and most people seemed certain the Americans would win because Jesse Owens was going to be one of their four runners. Owens has already done the seemingly impossible during the Games by winning three gold medals, for the hundred metres, the two hundred metres and the long jump.

"I wouldn't be too sure," said Tara. "Actually, from what I hear there's a bit of a scandal brewing. It depends who you believe. Apparently our coach has drafted in Owens and Metcalfe at the last moment even though they've not practised with the baton. Some people say they've dropped Glickman and Stoller to keep the Germans sweet. No prizes for guessing why ... they're Jewish of course..."

I avoided Sarah's eye as Tara said this.

"... But then by all accounts Hitler hasn't been so keen on a black man like Owens winning, so who can say? All I do know is, Owens and Metcalfe had better not drop that baton..."

They didn't, and the Americans won easily with the Germans taking a lucky bronze because the Dutch team themselves had an attack of butterfingers. The Führer slammed his fist down on the guard rail in frustration. A fourth gold medal for the black man Owens! Curses!

There was even more bad news for Hitler in the women's hundred metres relay. Firstly the much fancied Germans false-started, and then they too fumbled their baton changes to allow the Americans to lead home the British team (hurray!) and the Canadians. All three of us shouted and screamed as the runners on the final leg headed for the tape.

"We are just so good," said Tara complacently. However she got her comeuppance later when the British men beat the Americans in the four hundred metres relay. We hollered them home, and Tara was gracious enough to say our boys had run 'quite well'. It's been a wonderful, giddy afternoon, and so kind of Tara to think of us, but somehow, even out in the hot sunshine, the clouds of political unhappiness take the edge off the experience. If it's true that the Americans have given in about some of their own Jewish runners taking part, where does that leave Sarah? Mrs W. knows that she's Jewish, but does anyone else?

Wednesday 12th August 1936

We've slipped into a routine now. In the mornings we train – not in the Olympic pool any more, because that's in use for the competitions, but at 8.30 precisely a charabanc arrives to take us to an indoor pool a couple of miles away. Then in the afternoon we Do Things, arranged by Elke and her chums. On Monday it was a trip into Berlin to be walked around the streets and see the great buildings, none of whose names I can now remember. What stays in the mind are the pictures of the Führer (everywhere!). His eyes seem to follow you wherever you go. But the people seem smiling and happy, and Elke has been a perfectly nice companion providing we do as we're told. On Tuesday afternoon, we were informed, there was to be a barbecue with lots of German young people. I don't think either Sarah or I much wanted to go, and on Tuesday morning Sarah looked particularly out of sorts when we came back to the Reichssportfeld to smarten ourselves up after swimming.

"I thought Hanna and Jakob might have been in touch," she admitted. "I keep thinking that if we go off gallivanting I might miss them."

I sympathized and said I was sure they wouldn't just arrive without letting her know.

"Tara did," she said. "And anyway I don't know how easy it would be for them to get a letter to us here."

"Have you tried getting a message to them?"

"Well, I wrote before we left England to say I hoped we'd meet up. But otherwise no, I suppose not."

She moped around a bit over lunch, and then we set off reluctantly with Elke for the afternoon bash.

It was all rather strange. The hosts were what I at first thought were just German boy scouts, but when you looked more closely at their uniforms, you couldn't miss the inevitable swastikas among the more obviously scouty badges. They were very polite in offering us drinks and conversation, and actually much more relaxed than a crowd of English boys who were there. They were all hot and bothered in jackets, ties and polished black shoes.

"We're here on an exchange with a German school," hooted an English lad, "to improve our languages. I think we're rather overdressed, don't you? Gosh, you say you're with the Olympic team? Gosh! How fascinating!"

But fascinating or not, after that he didn't seem to have

anything more to say.

There were a few other girls too, standing around in small clumps looking bored and not talking to anyone. They looked sort of Spanish or Italian, so probably spoke neither German or English.

"Tell me, why are we here? What on earth is the point? I've got a perfectly good book back at the dormitory," Sarah raged.

"Extending the hand of international friendship," I answered, "At least, that's what Mrs Williams says. It's very nearly as important as swimming well, apparently."

"Well, I don't feel the least like extending a hand to anyone. Least of all the Hitler Youth. You know that's what they're called, don't you?"

I didn't, and hearing that snippet made me slightly keener to liven things up a bit. Like Sarah I was bored. It was quite difficult to shake off Elke though. She followed two steps behind us like a lost puppy.

"Did we talk to you earlier?" I said to one of a group of three rather shy-looking boy scouts. His name was Peter. "I can't remember. I'm afraid you all look rather the same, if you don't mind me saying..."

Sarah dug me in the ribs.

"Well it's true," I said. "It's the uniforms I suppose, and the fair hair."

"Thank you," he said, as if I'd offered him a compliment.

"Tell me," I went on, after a few more pleasantries, "I want

119

to know more about Germany. Sarah here is Jewish by birth. How are things for her fellow Jews in your country?"

I heard a little, sharp intake of breath from Sarah. Oh well, I'd done it now. One of the boys, shorter and more solid, clearly understood what I'd said. His face clouded over. Elke also looked shocked. Perhaps she'd not realised one of her charges was a Jew. She jumped in gamely, to try and avoid an international incident.

"In Germany," she said, "everyone has a chance to improve themselves and build a good life, provided they obey the laws."

The short boy looked at Elke dismissively, cleared his throat and spoke slowly.

"I do not know how it is in England," he said, "because I have never been there. But in Germany there have been problems with Jews. They are not always good citizens. They take money which is not theirs. They work against the interests of the people. When people do these kinds of things, they have to be taught how to behave. I'm sure it would be the same in your country. Don't you agree?"

"No," I said, angry to hear him putting the same arguments I'd heard at Seymour Lodge over dinner all those months ago. "No, actually I don't think we have any of those kinds of problems in Britain, but then I don't think our laws are quite the same as yours, from what I've heard ... about marriage, and work, and where we should live..."

The boy smiled unpleasantly. "Ah well," he said, and spread his hands. "Every nation must find its own solution, perhaps..." His companions looked embarrassed. Elke interrupted quickly now she had the opportunity of an awkward gap in the conversation.

"I think it is time for us to be going," she said. "Please come with me, Eleanor and Sarah."

When she had ushered us away from the boys she said crossly, "This was not a good chat, Eleanor. I am disappointed. We should I think always be polite with each other. Otherwise there may be things we should say to you which are also not so nice. For instance how Germany is still being punished after a war that is finished nearly twenty years ago, yes?"

"We're in the dog house," I said to Sarah later in the evening.

"We certainly are," she answered. "But at least you got us away from that dreadful party..." Sarah was still a bit mopey. The afternoon had done nothing to improve her state of mind, and not for the first time in my life, I was kicking myself for opening my big mouth.

Rather sullenly Elke showed up at breakfast today, bringing a message to say that Tara requested our attendance at the springboard diving this afternoon.

"A friend of mine's taking part," Tara said, as we found the seats which she'd so effortlessly managed to arrange.

(There seems to be no end to the strings Tara can pull!) "I don't think she'll get a medal, but she's just astonishing. Her name's Marjorie Gestring, and wait for it, she's just thirteen years old, although you'd never know it."

Tara was right. Marjorie Gestring is completely extraordinary. She's tall for her age, and her diving this afternoon was almost faultless, her entries to the pool leaving just the merest ripple despite the twists and turns which preceded them. The crowd took to her immediately and it seemed to inspire Marjorie to greater perfection with every dive, and at the same time to suck quality away from the performance of the favourite, another older, very glamorous American called Dorothy Poynton Hill. Tara pulled a face when Poynton Hill stepped onto the board.

"She spends far too much time looking in a mirror," she hissed. "Thinks she'll be in Hollywood this time next year!"

In fact Poynton Hill could only come third. Yet another American, Katherine Rawls, took the silver medal.

"Let's go and meet an Olympic champion," screamed Tara when the result was announced. And wouldn't you just know it, Marjorie turned out to be modest, nice and fun, as well as supremely talented. Some people have it all. It really isn't fair!

Thursday 13th August 1936

Well, here we are on the eve of The Big Day. Our slot tomorrow afternoon is after the men's backstroke final and just before the women's hundred metres relay, in which our girls say they're going to make a few people sit up and take notice. Let's hope we all do! We've pumped Mrs Williams for some information about the opposition but she can't, or won't, tell us very much.

"I've heard there's a good French girl, Sylvie Masteau, and of course the two Americans will be very strong. I see there's a Japanese lass, Yamada, and she's bound to be good, if she's anything like their men. But you know what I always say – swim your own race – and if you've got them in your sights over the last fifty, worry about them then. Just imagine you're back in St Pancras, ladies."

Which is all very well, but rather difficult, given the surroundings.

The other girls have been lovely, and say they'll all come down to give us a cheer, although really I think they'll only be there to support the relay swimmers. It's been odd for us and them: no one being very sure whether we're part of the team or not. They're all older than we are, although not by much – there are quite a few seventeen and eighteen-year-olds among our women, but they've all been concentrating on their events, and the fact Elke has been around so much, whisking us off hither and yon, has made it pretty obvious we're not really genuine team members, which is a bit of a shame. The girls mind their p's and q's too, not smoking in front of us, and keeping it among themselves if they nip out to meet one of the men. Gladys and Doris were great today though. Gladys said, "Now look you two. This British team has only been making up the numbers so far, and as for getting onto the podium we might have been trying to fly to the moon, so you're our best shot. We might get close in the relay, but we're depending on you to actually win something!"

Mother and Father have arrived safely and they took us out for tea today. They turned up in a grand-looking official car complete with a driver.

"The Embassy is looking after us very well," said my father, clearly very pleased at being chauffeured around. "And you made a particularly good impression on Sir Robert Vansittart, which helped somewhat!"

"Look at you," chorused the girls, when we came back afterwards. "Did you go somewhere posh?"

We did actually, with more chocolate cake on display than was fair the day before the most important race of one's life. We ate a little, extremely slowly, and Sarah was even more restrained than I was.

Talking of chocolate, we seem to have made our peace with Elke. She turned up this evening with two small boxes of chocolates just for us, and a card to wish us the best of luck in the race tomorrow. I'd wondered if she'd put in a bad report about us after the barbecue, but Mrs Williams hasn't said anything, so it seems not.

"Do you think we can allow ourselves one or two before bed?" Sarah asked.

"I won't," I said, "but you ate less cake than I did earlier on. I think you're allowed..."

Friday 14th August 1936

What a roller-coaster of a day! I was woken at about four in the morning by a tug on my sleeve from Sarah.

"I feel awful," she said. "I'm sure I'm going to be ill."

And she was, three times between then and about six o'clock, and fairly horribly too.

I was worried enough that in turn I woke Gladys.

"Oh my gawd," she said. "I thought it was too good to be true. I was expecting someone to go down with something. Thought it'd be me."

At eight Sarah was still sleeping, but her face was a ghostly white, far different from her normal rosy good health.

"Best leave her be," said Gladys. "We don't need to do anything for the moment. Plenty of time to get her up and running for later on. She'll be right as rain, you'll see."

But at midday when she tried to lever herself out of bed, Sarah was still weak and tearful.

"I'm not going to make it, Ellie," she wept. "Whatever am I going to do? What a waste! Oh, it's not fair!"

We tried to put her back together again, and console her by saying that it was just another race, and didn't mean anything, and she'd got all her best years ahead of her as a swimmer, but of course at that moment, and feeling as unwell as she did, it wasn't any help at all. Then came the dreadful moment when I had to pack my swimming togs and leave her behind in the dormitory to traipse up the gravel paths to the stadium with the others.

"You're a brilliant friend," she said to me just before I went. "You know that, don't you?"

I said that I did my best.

"So now you've got to go and swim for the two of us," she said. "And you deserve to win." She paused and then said quietly, "It was the chocolates, I reckon."

I looked at her as if she was mad. "More likely the water," I said. "Don't you think?"

"Well, where's Elke got to this morning then?" she asked.

126

"I knew there was something wrong as soon as I'd eaten them."

It was a very good question. In all the panic, I hadn't given Elke a thought. But they wouldn't do that, would they? Surely they wouldn't think it worthwhile to poison poor, gentle Sarah. Would they be that desperate to make sure it was a nice clean race, unsullied by the presence of a Jew in the water? My heart started to pound. It felt as if it was bouncing up and down inside my chest as I lagged behind the rest of the group. Suppose Sarah's suggestion was true, whatever should I do now? If I refused to swim, I'd bring down on my head all the disappointment and disapproval of the whole world, team members, Mrs Williams, school, parents, and perhaps even Sarah herself. But if I swam, wouldn't I be supporting a Fascist regime who were despicable enough to prevent a fifteen-year-old girl swimming in their country if she didn't fit into their stupid, crazy view of the way the world should be? But then again, was Sarah right? I stood with the other six swimmers, looking down the length of the vast stadium, waiting to be called to our marks, the deafening roar of the huge crowd filling my ears. The starter ordered us forward. My head spun and for a moment I thought I would lose my balance and simply topple into the water. The arena went silent. Every eye in the entire world seemed to be on me...

Sunday 10th August 1940

I'm home on a weekend's leave at Seymour Lodge, sleeping off a month of gruelling night shifts up at RAF Stanmore, where I'm doing things I can't speak to anyone about, not even Mother and Father. Careless talk costs lives, they tell us, so don't put even your nearest and dearest under pressure with stuff they'll only worry about. Father probably understands: maybe it's always been this way for him at the Foreign Office. It's so comforting to be back in my own little nest today, surrounded by the things and people I love the best. Mrs Etheridge still comes in to 'do', but the garden's too much for Bert now. Amy has left home and is working in a factory somewhere in Essex, so all in all Mother is pretty much running the house single-handed. I was tidying up and turning out some cupboards this morning, and then I found the old school exercise books filled with my scrawly fifth-form writing.

Why did I never finish the account of that day's events, and leave my story hanging so melodramatically? I was really, genuinely distressed, I think, believing that what I did then mattered. It was all about me, me, me – which is perhaps understandable if you're fifteen. And part of me felt ashamed that yes, in the end I did swim, and as soon as I hit the water all the years of training took over and for the duration of the race the doubts completely disappeared. A kind of anger that life could never be straightforward powered me on to a close second place behind one of the Americans, and a silver commemorative medal that still sits on the mantelpiece downstairs. It was a day of cheering and congratulations, of being toasted in lemonade and champagne. But as the thrill of the race subsided, it all left a slightly bitter taste.

I don't swim competitively any more, and neither does Sarah – though she kept going for a few more months after I stopped. I lost my appetite for all the long hours spent training my body because I became increasingly fascinated in what my mind could do. Mrs Williams and I never talked much about it, but I have a feeling that she understood why I let an obvious talent lapse, even if strangely Miss Bowes never really did – Miss Bowes having been the one most concerned that I shouldn't let swimming get in the way of academic study!

"A pity," she observed tartly at the end of my first year in the Sixth Form, "that it should be one thing or the other. Why not both?"

As it turns out, of course, the chance to swim in any Olympic Games this year, whether in London, Tokyo or anywhere else, vanished long ago. Instead of competing against the Germans we're at war with them now, fighting desperately for our lives so that Hitler's flags don't flutter down the length of Whitehall and over Buckingham Palace. The way things are going I shouldn't think there'll be any Games in 1944 either, or at least none that I'd want to take part in.

Was Sarah deliberately poisoned? I still find that rather hard to believe, and prefer to think it was bad luck, or as I said at the time, probably the water. As I wrote back then, Elke was always charming except on the occasion I made life hard for her. I notice now – though didn't then – the similarity between our names – Elke/Ellie! I've often wondered whether we might have been quite alike. What's she doing now, for instance? However, the fact remains that we didn't see her again before we left Berlin, which seems odd. There were no goodbyes or congratulations from her.

Leni Riefenstahl and her loverboy cameraman were at the race and although it may never see the light of day, I believe there's a more or less complete film of it including shots of me beforehand and afterwards. Because of her reputation as a champion of women's sport, she was the one to present the medals to us too, wearing trousers, albeit very chic trousers, which caused a real stir.

"I think she really is a man," said Gladys. "Like some of those hem-hem female German runners!"

"Maybe there will be a chance to meet the Führer in a little while," I remember Fräulein Riefenstahl saying to me after the presentation. I must have looked dubious. "He is a great man," she enthused. "He changes lives."

There probably was a reception with Hitler later in the day, but I wasn't there. I didn't want my life changed in that kind of way. I was more concerned with looking after Sarah.

She and I remain best friends. She works in her family's stationery business, which is now doing quite well, despite the war. She's talking about joining the army, which somehow doesn't seem right for such a kind, peaceful person. But then there's always been a very tough, almost angry side to Sarah, which no one sees at first.

Tara and her family are back in America, living in Washington DC. We still occasionally swap letters. She tells me that Harrison has no regular girlfriend and that he remembers me fondly. I tell her to forget it, that life here is seriously grim, and there's no time for that sort of thing. I think, all those thousands of miles away, she doesn't really understand how things are in Europe, although she might just be trying to cheer me up with her nonsense. Will the Americans come to help us, if things get worse? I don't know, but eventually they'll have to confront Hitler, even if it's in their own back yard. He believes he can rule the whole world and if he does, no one who is Jewish like Sarah, or black like Jesse Owens, or who just simply disagrees with him like me, will be safe.

The real reason I'm finishing the story off, and adding

this final diary entry, is that if I don't, you won't know the best thing about that occasion four years ago. By the Saturday morning Sarah was more or less back to her usual self after a day on bread and (boiled!) water, and it had always been arranged that we'd see Mother and Father a final time before they returned to England. They arrived mid-morning at the Reichssportfeld in the chauffeured car, and squeezed in with them and what seemed like a mountain of luggage were a middle-aged couple, the woman small, the man rather tall and stooped, both quietly dressed.

Sarah's eyes widened, and after a moment's astonished hesitation ran forward to embrace them. "Aunt Hanna, Uncle Jakob," she cried, "I'd given up on seeing you. How are you?"

Jakob's eyes twinkled. "We're very well," he said. "As well as you can possibly imagine. And even better for seeing you." I was immediately struck by his perfect English.

"Will you stay with us and have some lunch?" asked Sarah. "Oh, it is good to see you!"

"I'm afraid we can't," Jakob answered. "You see, we have an aeroplane to catch, and it would be a great shame if we missed it."

Sarah looked puzzled at first. Then her face lit up as she began to dare the impossible thought.

"We shall always be in debt to Mr Rhys Davies for his kindness," said Hanna.

My father shrugged as if to say it was nothing.

"No, truly. How will we ever be able to thank you enough?" Hanna continued, before turning back to Sarah. "We'll see you in London when you get home, my dear. Thanks to Ellie's father this is the start of a new life for us."

Not only had my father and mother found the money necessary to buy Jakob and Hanna's freedom from Germany, money which Sarah's own family couldn't raise, but part of my parents' plan had always been to use the Olympic Games to personally guarantee their safety by meeting them in Berlin and accompanying them home. It's a journey few Jews living under the Third Reich have been able to make. As our intelligence is beginning to indicate, countless more are now being forced to make far more sinister journeys out of Germany to the Jewish ghettos in occupied Poland at Lodz and Warsaw. Who knows what will eventually happen to them there? From some of the reports I have seen coming through Stanmore, we should be very afraid for them. If life under German rule was bad for Jews in 1936, it's infinitely worse now.

Hanna and Jakob now also work in the Rosenthal family business. They're regular visitors to Seymour Lodge, always bringing Mother and Father some little present or other. Jakob plays the piano in our front room occasionally, and is trying to help Mother learn to play a little better. They still look stricken and guilty when they tell us about the horrors from which they've escaped: news of their old friends somehow reaches them from time to time, and it's never good.

I now think there are some things in life you just can't know: all you can do is be your best self, flip a coin, and hope that you're doing the right thing. Whether it was better to keep talking to the Germans and playing sport against them in 1936 I have no idea. It may have done good: it may have done harm. But by 1938 when Chamberlain came back from Munich waving a piece of paper, and claiming that he'd done a deal with Hitler, I for one thought he was wrong and that war was inevitable. The time for talking had passed some time previously. What will happen to us all from here on it's impossible to say, but I do know this. We're dealing with a monster whose head must be cut off. For my part, I'm doing whatever I can to fight him, every bit as much as if I were a man. That's the legacy of my time at CCS. Miss Bowes, I will make you proud of me yet!

Historical note

How far back in human history do we have to go to find the first sporting contests? It is not difficult to imagine even primitive Stone Age people testing each other out to see who could run quickest or throw a rock the furthest. Although humans certainly have to cooperate with each other to survive, the desire to compete with each other is pretty basic too, and some people will claim that this urge is written into our genes.

Certainly, by the time proper history is being written, in the fifth century BCE civilization of the ancient Greeks, a regular set of organized games brought people together at Olympia on the Peloponnesian peninsula. Even earlier than that, Homer's great poem, *The Iliad*, possibly written in about 800 BCE, gives an account of chariot racing, boxing, wrestling, running, archery and javelin-throwing in the aftermath of the Trojan War supposedly centuries before he wrote.

Two ideas crop up very early in the history of sport. One is that a sporting contest must always be fair – which sometimes still causes difficulty and controversy.

For instance, is it OK for the South African champion paralympic runner Oscar Pistorius to run on his 'blades' against competitors in ordinary running shoes? The other idea is that sport can be some kind of a useful substitute for war – that it can bring people together and contribute to peace-making and understanding. But at what point should you refuse to compete against an individual or a country whose ideals and way of life you think are wrong? That's what this book is mostly about. It's a debate that was widely aired before the 1936 Berlin Olympics, nearly causing the American team not to attend, and the same arguments were raised before the 2008 Beijing Olympic Games, because many people believed the government of China was continuing to oppress its people.

Perhaps you will remember the intensity of the competition to stage the next two football World Cups. These days all governments want to show off their countries to the rest of the world in the best possible light. To put it another way, you might say governments want to use sporting occasions like the World Cup and the Olympic Games as 'propaganda'. The 1936 Olympics are important because Hitler's Germany under Minister of Information Joseph Goebbels was perhaps the first government to do this in a systematic way. Goebbels understood that for the first time the growing popularity of 'moving pictures' and radio made it possible for people all around the world to follow the action. The aim was to show how wonderful life in National Socialist Germany was and how much better than anywhere else. Of course that meant it was important for Hitler to cover up anything bad, like for instance the evil things that were being done to Jewish people. Even so some of his craziness about matters of racial purity quickly became obvious – for instance, the idea that fair headed 'Aryan' Germans were really descended from one of the ancient Greek tribes. He thought Greece had been taken over by a 'foreign' race of dark swarthy people who bore no relation to the original ancient Greeks. Because he believed that Germans were the true heirs of the Greek tradition, he hoped that Berlin would become the permanent base for the Olympic Games.

The modern Olympic Games were founded in 1896, through the inspiration of Baron Pierre de Coubertin, a Swiss nobleman, which is why the home of the International Olympic Committee is still in Lausanne, Switzerland. He may have got his idea from the 'Olympian Games' that he saw take place in the English village of Much Wenlock a few years earlier (they're still held there annually).

Those 1896 Games were held in Athens with just twelve different nations competing. Fittingly, the winner of the first Marathon event was a Greek called Spiridon Louis. (You could perhaps use a search engine to learn the fascinating story of how this event came to be included.) Subsequently the Games were held every four years, and rather against the wishes of the Greek government they were staged not in Athens, but in important cities in different parts of the world: Paris in 1900, St Louis, Missouri in 1904, London in 1908 and so on.

The 1916 Games should have gone to Berlin, but not surprisingly the Great War prevented that from happening. As one small part of the punishment meted out by the Allies when the war ended, Germany was forbidden even from taking part in 1920 and 1924. Once they were re-admitted in 1928, the successful campaign to bring the Games to Berlin in 1936 began.

In the light of everything that happened later it's very important to remember how the German authorities resented their treatment after the Great War. Germany had to pay damagingly large amounts of money at a time when the whole world was in a great economic depression. Its economy probably suffered worse than anywhere else. People were poor, often unemployed and unhappy. The political instability this caused created the conditions for the rise of fascism, and for Hitler to take eventual complete power as dictator. The strength of his government was to put Germans back into jobs. They began to see possible material rewards for themselves as great state buildings and roads were built, foreign holidays were promised, and Germany's armed forces were built up again. Having promoted the self-interest of his people in this way, Hitler was able to lead them into the disastrous international adventures which followed.

His ideas, including his prejudice against Jews, struck a chord with people in other countries too. Oswald Mosley founded the British Union of Fascists, one of whose demonstrations in the East End of London you can read about in this book. Mosley and Diana Guinness (born Mitford) were married after the Olympics in October 1936 at Goebbels' house in Berlin, with Hitler as a guest. Fascism found favour with many British people in high places, including perhaps some members of the royal family.

The 1936 Games are perhaps best remembered for the achievement of the black American athlete Jesse Owens. Much to the obvious annoyance of Hitler, Owens won four gold medals – the one hundred and two hundred metres sprints, the 4 x 100 relay, and the long jump. Hitler regarded black people, like Jews, as inferior. He wondered aloud whether it was fair that they should compete against white (Aryan) people.

Hitler's invasions of Europe, and the gradual spread of the 1939 war around the world meant that again, there were no Olympic Games in 1940 or indeed 1944, as Ellie guesses towards the end of the book. The first Games after the war came to London in 1948. 2012 will see them in Britain for a third time. They're extremely unlikely to come back in our lifetime.

Ellie, Sarah, Tara and their families are all inventions of mine. There was no swimming invitation event at 1500 metres for women in the 1936 Olympics: it wasn't a distance that women then swam. The other swimmers I mention in the book all really did take part in the Games, but British swimming wasn't really competitive in world terms back then, and no medals of any colour were won. However a number of our swimmers managed sixth places, including Doris Storey, Lorna Frampton and Bobby Leivers.

The details you'll have read about North London life in 1935, and at a girls' school of the same period are hopefully accurate. Camden Collegiate School never existed as such, but there were and are splendid schools of this character not many miles away. My special thanks go to the staff and pupils of the North London Collegiate School for allowing me to raid their archive.

Similarly my account of life for the women competitors in Berlin is based on historical record. Today's athletes certainly wouldn't put up with such conditions or the inequality between the men's accommodation and the women's. On the other hand this was a time that was important for the growth of women's sport. In many ways it was then in its infancy: many men still saw women's athletic ability or display as 'unladylike', more than two thousand years after the Greeks first introduced regular running competitions for women.

Our sporting heroes put themselves through countless

hours of tedium and more pain than most of us could live with. So it's perhaps no surprise that sometimes they don't want to concern themselves with the politics which often arise when they compete abroad. These days of course sportsmen and sportswomen may eventually make a fortune from what they do – which was even the case occasionally back in 1936. Is it all right to disengage our sporting brains in the face of a suffering world? If you'd been Ellie or Sarah, what would you have done?

Here's a sneak peek at
the latest exciting My Story:

WARTIME PRINCESS

June 1st 1939

This is the first ever diary of Her Royal Highness, Princess Margaret Rose.

Sometimes I wake early and can't get back to sleep, because my head's too full of things I want to do. So I thought it would be nice to have something to do that doesn't make a noise. I'm always getting told off for too much noise.

I have this chunky notebook with a photo of me and my sister, Lilibet, on the front. There are no dates in it, so it's not a proper diary, but that's good. It means I don't have to write in it every day. I get a bit fed up with things I have to do. There are far too many of those.

Ruby and Bobo, our nursery maids, and Allah, our nanny, are fast asleep. So is my sister.

Lilibet is Her Royal Highness, Princess Elizabeth, and she is a Very Important Person, because one day she'll be the Queen of England. Poor her, that's what I say.

She'll be a very good queen, because she's a very good person. She's sensible and obedient, and everyone considers her responsible and serious.

She's not a bit like me!

June 21st

Oh dear, I'm not very organized about this diary business. It's weeks since I started it. But while Mummy and Papa have been away in Canada and America, our governess, Crawfie, has kept us so busy. Lilibet thinks Crawfie does it so we won't miss Mummy and Papa too much, but they've been gone more than six weeks. That's a long time to be without your mother and father. But when your parents are the King and Queen of England, you must expect sad times and just keep smiling. It isn't always easy.

We have lessons, of course, and walks, but we've also had lots of outings to keep us cheerful. The best ones were a boat trip on the River Thames, visits to the Royal Tournament and the Royal Mint (we were presented with some special coins), and some glorious picnics.

The most exciting outing was a ride on an underground train! Lilibet and I call it the tube, because that's what the people who use it every day call it. I tried to pretend I was a working lady, but it was difficult because there were policemen with us, and photographers kept calling out. Crawfie was very proper and just walked us straight through the crowd. I was allowed to hold my own ticket.

But there's another exciting outing planned for early tomorrow! Mummy and Papa are sailing home and we are to sail to meet them!

I can't wait.

June 22nd

I'm supposed to be resting for ten minutes while Mummy and Papa say goodbye to the captain of this ship. It's called *Empress of Britain*, which is sort of what Mummy is!

This morning Lilibet and I sailed on a Royal Navy destroyer called HMS *Kempenfelt*. It was so exciting when at last we saw Mummy and Papa waving to us. We were so happy to see them again – so happy I almost forgot to curtsey! I'm glad I remembered, because lots of people were watching. Mummy always says it's important for us to behave properly in public. Lilibet never makes a mistake, but then, she always behaves properly, even in private.

When we were alone, we had such hugs! Papa said I've grown, which I'm pleased about. It's not nice being the smallest person in the palace.

Everyone talked at once, and then it was lunchtime.

The ship's saloon was decorated with dozens of balloons. It was so bright and happy. And that was just how I felt inside – full of balloons!

The captain took us on to the bridge as we sailed towards the harbour. The bridge is where they drive the ship. It looked very complicated, but I didn't have a chance to examine all the dials and buttons. Papa drew Lilibet and me forward so we could join them in waving to all the people who had come to welcome him and Mummy home.

It looks as if every person in Britain has come to Southampton!

Next we're travelling to London by train.

June 23rd

Crawfie came and spoke to Allah this morning. I was so tired I could hardly open my eyes.

Then Allah whispered, 'No lessons this morning, Margaret.' She's allowed to call me 'Margaret' in private. 'Her Majesty told Miss Crawford you need to rest.'

I suddenly remembered yesterday. I leapt out of bed and ran to shake Lilibet. 'Wake up! Let's go and see Mummy and Papa!'

She sat up. 'May we, Allah?'

Allah nodded. 'His Majesty sent a message to say he can't wait to see his girls!'

What fun we had! It was just like in the old days in our house in Piccadilly, before Papa became King and we moved to Buckingham Palace. Lilibet's too grown up for pillow fights (she's thirteen), but I'm not!

It's so lovely to have us four all together. Papa couldn't stop grinning as we rode home in the carriage from the station yesterday. I was silly to think that every person in Britain was in Southampton. There were thousands more on the London pavements. Mummy said her arm ached from waving. I don't know how she manages to keep smiling without stopping. I can't. It makes my face ache. Also, Lilibet and I rode facing backwards, which always makes me feel peculiar, what with the carriage bouncing and the horses' heads bobbing as the guardsmen ride alongside. Then it was upstairs for a balcony appearance.

Before we stepped on to the balcony, Lilibet said, 'Remember not to push to the front, Margaret. The people have come to see Mummy and Papa, not us.'

She shoved me in the right direction. Helpful, but irritating. I got my own back by being last to leave the balcony, and turning to give the people a final wave. Lilibet kept smiling, but I think she was annoyed.

June 27th

Lilibet knows about my diary. She came up behind me while I was lying on the floor, writing. She didn't say anything, and she's never mentioned it. See? She's such a good person. I'd have asked about it if it had been hers, and I know my fingers would have been itching to get hold of it. But not Lilibet. She tries so hard to behave well, and she'd think it was sneaky to take a peek.

But still, I'll keep it hidden. These are my true thoughts, and I'm sure there'll be some I'd rather people didn't see.

I must change now for swimming. We're entering some races at the Swimming Bath Club in Mayfair on Thursday. It's fun there, because we swim with other children. We're usually allowed time to just mess around, as Ruby calls it, and it's so much better when there's more than two of us. Lilibet says I shouldn't grumble about us being alone, because we're fortunate to have our own swimming pool here in the palace. Most children only go to the public baths – if they're lucky. I didn't think about that until she said it.

Later

We did really well, considering we're not used to racing. Mummy presented the prizes, of course, and there were lots of photographs. All those flashing lights! I got a silver cup and Lilibet got a shield. We were going to put them on the nursery mantelpiece, but Papa said they must have pride of place in the drawing room. He's such a darling.

Wouldn't it be lovely if every country had a king like Papa? I feel sorry for the German people. They don't have a king or queen. Instead they have a leader called Herr Adolf Hitler. Although Mummy and Papa don't discuss him much, one of the footmen, who we really like, said, 'I expect His Majesty will talk about nothing else but Herr Hitler when he meets the prime minister today.' He was taking the dogs for a run and Lilibet and I tagged along. Not everybody likes our corgis, because they can be snappy, but he does. He takes a ball and plays with them. That's why we like him. I call him Buttons, because he looks just like Buttons in my *Cinderella* book.

Lilibet said, 'Herr Hitler's a bad man, isn't he?' and Buttons said, 'He's bad for Germany, that's for sure, Ma'am, and he's bad news for us, he is. That's if there's a war.'

War. Ugh. Horrid word.

After tea, Lilibet and I went upstairs to groom our horses. We keep them on the nursery landing. Some are on wheels, and some stand on their own four legs. They all have saddles and bridles. We groom them all every evening, and feed them and give them water. Well, not really, of course, just pretend. We know how to do it properly, because we watch the grooms look after our ponies when we've been riding.

Actually, Lilibet sometimes sits on the floor with her back against the wall and cuddles Dookie or Jane or one of the other dogs. She doesn't play much these days. It's because she's almost grown up. She even wears silk stockings, instead of socks. I'm glad I don't, because I'd rip them to shreds in no time. But what fun to be grown up. Parties, music and dancing, and lovely clothes, too. And visits to the ballet!

July 15th

We're off to sea again! Papa says the royal yacht is almost as old as he is, and this is probably our last chance to sail in her. We're going to visit the Royal Naval College at Dartmouth, in Devon, where Papa did part of his naval training.

July 22nd

We've had a lovely trip so far, except that Lilibet and I are expected to carry on with lessons while we're travelling. Honestly, we never get a holiday from work. Lilibet groaned when she realised it was arithmetic first (she didn't let Crawfie hear), so I decided to waste time. 'Crawfie,' I said, 'I simply must tell you about my dream last night!'

The dream was actually quite dull, and I can hardly remember it. But I did what Crawfie always tells me to do, and used my imagination. She kept saying, 'Oh, Margaret, do stop,' and, 'Margaret, don't be ridiculous,' but I know she enjoyed my tale. Lilibet struggled not to laugh, because she knew what I was up to. It worked. We wasted nearly half the lesson!

Later on some of the officers taught us a dance called the Lambeth Walk. The best bit was that every time the words went '... doing the Lambeth Walk', we all had to shout 'Oy!' They said I picked up the steps really quickly. I think Lilibet did, too. When they taught us another dance, the Palais Glide, we joined together and danced in a row. It was more difficult than the Lambeth Walk. Lilibet did better than me because she concentrates more than I do, but we both ended up laughing at the way our legs kept getting muddled.

The ship sailed into the River Dart, and we moored near Dartmouth Castle. Our ship, the *Victoria and Albert*, is surrounded all the time by dozens of sailing and rowing boats. They look like toys compared to our ship. They're full of friendly people, waving and cheering. Dartmouth is a pretty village, with painted cottages clinging to the hillside. I wanted to leap ashore and run up the hill, but we had to be received officially at the castle's quay. Lots of hands to shake. As usual, I was the last in the shaking-hands line. Papa's first, being the King, then Mummy, then Lilibet – partly because she's older than me, but especially because she's the heir to the throne. As I said, she's a Very Important Person. I'm just number two in line for the throne.

Tomorrow we visit the college. Papa's second cousin, Uncle Dickie – he's really Lord Louis Mountbatten – is dining on board tonight.

July 23rd

What a lovely day! It's been so much fun. Lilibet says it's been one of the nicest days she's ever had in her life. (And I know why!!!)

As it's Sunday, we were supposed to attend a service in the college chapel, but Uncle Dickie sent a message saying that Lilibet and I shouldn't go, because some of the cadets have mumps. I once saw someone with mumps, and it wasn't a pretty sight. He had great swellings each side of his face, and Mummy said the poor boy felt really ill. I don't want that. What's worse is you have to stay indoors for absolutely ages, resting, which would be ghastly.

So off Mummy and Papa went, escorted by some very smart cadets. They're young men who are training to become naval officers.

Lilibet and I were taken to the Captain's House to wait for our parents. The captain's the person in charge of the college. His family are the Dalrymple-Hamiltons, who we haven't met before.

We both felt shy, being in a strange place, but we were introduced to a tall, fair-haired cadet, called Prince Philip of Greece and Denmark. Uncle Dickie had sent him to the Captain's House to amuse us. He's a second or third cousin of ours – I can never work them out, but Queen Victoria is his ancestor, which is the same as us. She's our great-great-grandmother.

To be honest, I think Philip's a bit of a show-off. But it doesn't matter, because he's good fun. He got the Dalrymple-Hamiltons' train set going, and both Lilibet and I had lots of goes. Afterwards, we went for a walk, and when we reached the tennis court, Philip said, 'Let's jump the net!'

I would have had a go, but it was too high and, anyway, we weren't wearing the sort of clothes you can jump nets in. Lilibet wouldn't have jumped it, whatever she was wearing, not at any price. She doesn't do that sort of thing. But Philip did! Over and over he jumped (showing off).

He's a bit of a tease, and he kept picking on me. I didn't mind. He makes me laugh.

We played croquet, too. It was so draughty up on the hill that we had to keep our coats on. Lilibet's a good player – it's quite hard to be bad at croquet – and she thought Philip was good, too. She kept watching him. In my opinion he cheated, and I told her so.

'He isn't cheating,' she hissed. 'Don't be so rude, Margaret.'

I watched his mallet and his feet, not his face, and I say he cheated. Still, everyone cheats at croquet, don't they? It's part of the fun.

Philip was invited to lunch, and he was friendly with everyone. Mummy said, 'You've met Elizabeth before, Philip, at the wedding of her uncle George, the Duke of Kent. Do you remember?'

'Of course I do, Ma'am,' he said, but he changed the subject quickly, so I don't think that was true. After all, she was only four. Why would he remember her?

Later that evening, I said to Lilibet, 'Wouldn't it be lovely if Philip lived in London? We could become friends.'

She went pink and said, 'Yes, that would be nice.'

I looked her right in the eye until she couldn't help laughing. She really likes Philip, I can tell.

July 24th

Prince Philip joined us for dinner on the *Victoria and Albert* last night. Either they don't feed the cadets very well, or that boy has the most enormous appetite! He ate and ate and finally polished off a huge banana split. He even finished before me!

Lilibet and I talked in bed last night.

'He's a very good-looking boy, isn't he?' she said.

In fact, she talked about him quite a bit. It's odd, because he's not the sort of person she normally likes. He's bouncy and, well, boisterous, Crawfie says. Lilibet usually likes calm, quiet people. Except for me. I'm not usually calm or quiet, and she loves me.

Experience history first-hand with My Story –
a series of vividly imagined accounts of life in the past.

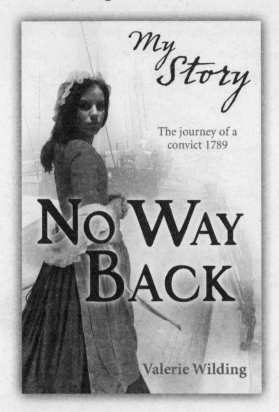

My Story

The journey of a
convict 1789

No Way Back

Valerie Wilding

It's 1789. Poor **Mary Wade** envies the
rich people who toss her a halfpenny just to go away.
One day **she makes a mistake** that lands her in
London's filthiest prison. Mary's one chance of
escaping the gallows is a long and **perilous
journey** to the other side of the world.
What choice does she have when
there is no way back?

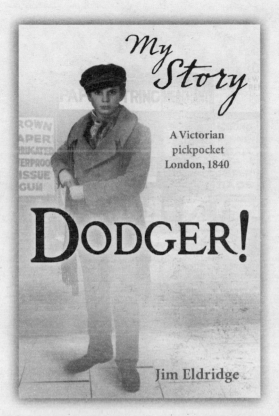

My Story

A Victorian
pickpocket
London, 1840

DODGER!

Jim Eldridge

In 1840, **Dick Maybury** arrives in
London with nowhere to stay, **no money**
and no friends. A chance meeting with the
Adelphi gang gives him all three. But the
gang make their living **outside the law**
and Dick learns that, once begun,
**the life of a pickpocket
is very hard to leave behind...**

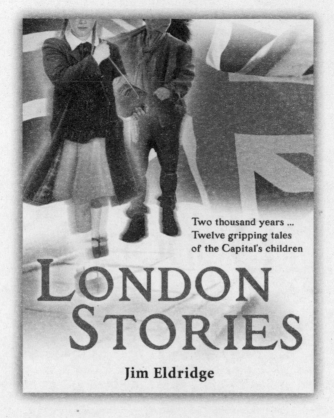

Two thousand years ...
Twelve gripping tales
of the Capital's children

LONDON STORIES

Jim Eldridge

No city has as many amazing stories to tell as
London. Brought low by the Black Death, burned to
the ground, and blitzed ... London always rises from
the ashes and new generations of children are born
to make its history.

Let twelve of these children lead you on an
incredible journey from a simple Saxon settlement
by the Thames to a vibrant, global city hosting the
2012 Olympic Games.